Vrooms, Brooms, & Heirlooms

Witchy Business Mysteries Book 1

Maddy Savanna

Contents

Chapter One

He Who Only Comes Out At Night

MOST DAYS, I COULD tell what was wrong with a car based on the sound it made as it rolled to a stop in front of Sunray's Auto Shop. Judging from the wheezing, groaning squawk currently outside, it was going to need an exorcism.

"Yikes," I muttered to the oil reservoir cap I was unscrewing under the raised hood of a Mazda.

"Probably took it to Speedy Zone," Boxy, my co-conspirator/co-manager, called from...somewhere. Even with his cane, he moved stealthily, like a sixty-something-year-old ninja wearing overalls. He'd been working on the Chevrolet next to me not two seconds ago.

"Boxy?" I asked, glancing around. "You here, or did I dream you up?"

He reappeared from behind the Chevrolet and winked with the only eye he could wink with. The other was made of glass. He liked to take it out sometimes to let my cat familiar, Professor Studmuffin Salvitore III, play with it, which...sure. Why not?

"Better take a picture to prove that dreams really do come true," Boxy said.

"I'll get right on that." I grinned and pointed to a red-striped quart of oil on the shelf next to his head. "Hand me the high-mileage oil?" I turned back to the Mazda, and when my favorite ninja didn't deliver, I glanced over and did a double-take at the velocity of Boxy's jaw dropping to his knees.

"Vic," Boxy whispered to me, "it's him."

"Him who?"

"He Who Only Comes Out at Night," Boxy hissed, his gaze pinned to the windows of the garage.

He Who Only Comes Out At Night was Boxy's nickname for the new owner/manager of Speedy Zone across town, Travis Black. I knew him when we were little. I also knew his dad, and that was bad enough. Speedy Zone had re-opened about two months ago, complete with bikini-clad women washing cars and coupon booklets to help draw customers. I knew all of this because those same customers came to Sunray's Auto Shop shortly after. The hocus-pocus they'd gotten at Speedy Zone hadn't fixed their cars. That was some stellar managing, especially since no one ever saw Travis except at night. So, had he invested in some SPF 10,000 to grace us with his presence before the sun went down?

"Checking out his competition, probably," I muttered.

Professor Studmuffin Salvitore III slipped into the garage part of the shop from the waiting room door, the smell of his three-layer chocolate buttercream cake drifting in after him. My stomach grumbled. That would be dinner later. Maybe even dessert. Part familiar, part baker, all cattitude, the handsome tom strolled across the cement floor to investigate.

"Not too close, Studmuffin," Boxy warned.

The cat turned and gave him serious stink-eye for questioning his judgement.

I snorted a laugh.

The demon-possessed car outside cut its engine. A long shadow slanted across the sidewalk outside.

"Quick." Boxy pulled his large blue-and-white striped railroad cap low over his face as if hoping it would swallow him. "He's coming. What do we do?"

"Uh, hand me the quart of high-mileage oil?"

He pointed at me with his cane. "Yes. Act natural. Where is it again?"

Footsteps approached outside.

"Behind you on the shelf to your...left."

He shuffled right, the fingers not on his cane waving into jazzy grabby hands.

I pressed my hand to my thigh to make the letter L to be sure I was correct. I often confused left and right because of my dyslexia. "Other left."

"Bah!" He stabbed his cane into the ground to jazz his way in the other direction.

I hid my grin behind my shirt collar. It was ninja crazy town in the shop, our normal, and I loved every second of it.

He handed me the quart just as the door to the shop opened and dinged the overhead bell.

I turned and looked, my curiosity about why Travis was here getting the better of me. My gaze stuck briefly to his broad chest. He was tall with short sandy-blond hair, late thirties, and two spurs and a hat away from full-on cowboy if his boots were any indication. Worn jeans and a red flannel completed his ensemble. He also wore a big blue ring on his index finger that appeared to glow slightly. Maybe it was just the sunset streaming through the windows playing tricks with my eyes though.

I allowed myself a second to drink him in for a beat while the urge to tell him to get lost tipped my tongue. If he'd grown up to be anything like his dad, I already didn't like him.

"So..." Without glancing at either Studmuffin right at his feet, Boxy, or me, he threw an utter look of disdain around the shop. "This is Sunray's."

A simmer started low in my gut from that look alone, so I dismissed his existence by leaning over the oil reservoir with the quart and my tongue firmly planted between my teeth.

"Hey there. Boxy here." Boxy limped past me, wiping his free hand down the front of his overalls, and then thrust it toward Travis.

"I don't know what that is," he said, his voice gravelly as if roughened by sleep.

"It's a hand. You shake it," Boxy said, his sarcasm on full drip.

"I mean Boxy."

"Oh, that's my name. Or that's what my friends call me."

I could hear Boxy's mind working to determine whether to give his real name or not, something he usually reserved for lawyers or politicians.

"Do you always keep it so messy in here?" Travis asked.

A low hiss seeped through my clenched teeth over the *glug-glug* of oil. This shop charged my blood, was my home. Hearing someone like him, some rando who didn't know anything about cars come in and ridicule it, made me want to high-five his face with a metal chair. I straightened, turned, and sliced him with the sharpest glare I could muster.

He met my fury with wide, hazel eyes, side-lit from the sun to a mossy green color. They tracked over my turquoise ponytail, my black tank top underneath my open work shirt, my plaid shorts, and down to my steel-toed work boots.

"If you're here to get your car fixed, we can do it," I said, snapping his gaze back to mine instead of vacationing over the rest of me with the tone of my voice. "Otherwise, you can go now."

He pointed at me but turned to Boxy. "You let customers in here work on their own cars?"

Just like the hundreds of times before I'd heard a comment like that, I gathered it up between my knuckles and crushed it. My boiling simmer cranked high and fizzed underneath my skin, growing especially hot under the collar of my work shirt that clearly read sunray's Auto Shop. Only not so clearly when I glanced down. More like su Ay to p with all the oil stains.

Boxy slapped his hand to his forehead and dragged it down his whiskered chin. "Oh, you've done it now, boy-o."

"Meow," Studmuffin agreed and licked one of his white murder mittens.

I stepped closer to Mr. Speedy Zone, close enough to see the golden spokes flecking his green eyes and the dark shadows underneath. "There are two car shops in town," I started, my voice measured but with just enough bite to drive my point home right between his blond eyebrows. "Yours and this one.

And since you've opened yours, we've never been busier. People come here when they actually want to get their cars fixed."

"Amen," Boxy muttered and gave the sign of the cross to the holy car gods.

"Tell me, which shop do you take your car to?" I asked Travis.

His green eyes narrowed, then tracked down again to the shop's smudged name stitched to my shirt. He held out his hand. "I'm Travis."

Since he was introducing himself, he obviously didn't remember me. I backed off and jazzed my hands Boxy-style so Travis would see that actually fixing cars made me not fit for touching. Ever. Especially by him. "My friends call me Vic. You can call me Victoria."

"*You're* Victoria?" He nodded as if something had just clicked into place. "That makes sense, but wow, you've changed. Are you always like this with everyone who walks in here?"

Boxy rocked back on his heels and muttered, "Yes."

I shot him a mock hurt look. No way could I ever really get mad at Boxy. "Like what?"

"So..." Travis winced as if rattling around a whole toolbox of possibilities in that head of his, most of which I probably didn't want to hear. "Spicy."

I snorted. "Only toward rude people who come in here to cast judgement on this shop when they absolutely have no right to. Otherwise, I'm the least spicy person you'll ever meet."

He smiled and somehow made it look skeptical. "Is that right?"

"That's right."

"Well, then." He bowed his head, his gaze never leaving mine. "I'm sorry I was rude."

I shrugged. "Apology accepted if you get your car exorcised soon."

"Exorcised?" He chuckled, a low, pleasant sound.

"She's a tad obsessed with ghosts and spooky things," Boxy said, hiking his thumb toward me. "Too much TV, this one."

I snorted at the King of Horror Movies, who fed my addiction with his impressive stash of old DVDs. The witchy ones were my favorites.

Studmuffin blinked sleepily up at Travis. Poor thing must've needed a nap after his long day of naps.

"So. The reason I'm here." Travis fished some folded-up papers out of his back pocket. "You two have probably heard about the mini-mall that's coming to town?"

Oh yes. The mini-mall. It was a rumor that had bred conspiracy theories about Belle's Cove, our small coastal town in Georgia, becoming more like a city. The worry was that if Belle's Cove grew larger, it would have all the same problems of cities like crime and road rage due to increased traffic. The exact same concerns had cropped up when Safe-Mart had been built about twenty years ago, so I'd heard. As far as I knew, the only thing that made people criminals or ragey was the one open check-out lane among a seemingly endless row of closed check-out lanes.

"Yeah," I said, posting my hands on my hips. "My microwave may have mentioned a mini-mall to me."

Boxy shot me a grin. "Was that before or after the weekly world alien-sighting report at eleven?"

"Before," I joked. "Keep up."

Boxy chuckled and shook his head. "Been hearing about that mini-mall for years. Nothing's ever come out of it."

"Until now." Travis ticked his gaze between us, a frown creasing his forehead. "Despite what your microwave may have told you... Whatever that means. It just so happens that construction starts in a couple months on the empty lot next to Speedy Zone."

"Right next door?" I quirked an eyebrow. "Well, congratulations. You'll be a lot busier."

"The shop could become a lot busier a lot sooner with the right person calling the shots." Travis handed me the papers.

I took them, trying to read his blank expression and decipher the words he'd just said. A sudden tremor started in my hands, and a sour taste slid to the back of my tongue. Whatever these papers said, I was pretty sure I wouldn't like it. I glanced down, and the words swam over the page, the letters rearranging themselves into nonsense. If I concentrated, I could read them, but not right then, not in front of him where he could watch me closely.

"Give me the condensed version," I said, gazing up at him again.

"It's my offer to you. A generous deal for you to buy Speedy Zone from me. I'll make sure you have everything you need to meet the growing demand from the mini-mall."

Boxy growled. Studmuffin snored. Travis didn't seem to notice the ball of fur that had fallen asleep on his left boot.

"What?" I demanded. "You want me to buy your shop? From *you*?"

"Well..." Travis glanced at Boxy, who gave him no love in return. "Yeah. Look, I know what my dad did—" He broke off, likely at the projection of rage, much stronger than that for one open check-out lane, written all over my face.

He didn't know anything about anything. My dad had started Speedy Zone with Marcus Black, Travis's dad. Marcus liked to do business as shady as possible and pulled the financial rug out from under my dad by stealing from the company. With most of his money now gone and with a young daughter to raise, my dad started again from scratch with this shop, Sunray's. Growing up, I was the one who had attached myself to his hip since I could walk and had learned everything there was to know about cars. Now, I managed Sunray's the best I could with Boxy's help. My dad had handed the shop over to me shortly after he'd met and married a sugar momma and was now honeymooning the world with her. Which, good for him. He deserved all of his happiness. I told him so as often as I could.

But hearing Travis's offer to buy back the company that should've belonged to Dad anyway felt like a slap to the face.

"...and you can stick it where the sun don't shine, you filthy blood sucker," Boxy was saying, his voice snapping sharp like a rubber band.

Travis raised his hands to ward off Boxy's wrath. "I'll leave the paperwork here. How about you two think on it."

Boxy pointed to the door with his cane. "How about you see yourself out."

Nodding, Travis settled his green gaze on me once again. "Just...think about it."

I looked away, shaking my head. Buying another business? I might as well have been chasing Boxy's glass eyeball into uncharted territory. I had no idea if that was, or would ever be, a good business deci-sion.

My mind flashed the college application lying next to my unopened grimoire on my kitchen table. Those things had been waiting for close to twenty years. The whole table had become The Place To Put Things I Don't Want To Think About Today. Maybe business school would help me make these types of decisions, though. Maybe it wouldn't, but I would offer up a kidney to have the savvy to keep this place around for the next forty-plus years. But two shops? Maybe more eventually?

The ambition and the car know-how had never been what held me back. It was my dyslexia and my failed witch status. All of my doubts centered around those things. Always had.

"We can't be persuaded so easily," Boxy snapped. "I know, the nerve of us. How dare you try to sell something to us that Vic's dad bled his whole life into."

To his credit, Travis gently removed himself from underneath my sleeping familiar. Then he turned and sighed, placing the papers on top of the empty oil quarts and other trash. Fitting spot. His shoul-ders filled the doorframe as he left. Seconds later, his car screamed to life. I could almost hear the pea soup gurgling under the hood in preparation for a purge, hopefully right into Travis's face.

"Vic?" Boxy asked. "What's going on in that head?"

I shook it, trying to rattle out a coherent thought. "I think He Who Only Comes Out At Night should only come out at night."

Chapter Two

Professor Studmuffin Salvitore III & Someone Else's Murder Mittens

STUDMUFFIN ADOPTED ME ABOUT five months ago when he appeared inside Sunray's, strode through the shop like he owned the place, and then immediately started baking for my customers. As cats sometimes do.

Like I did with all animals, I'd melted into a puddle, completely smitten. He had stunning yellow-green eyes, a white chest and white murder mittens, and sleek black and white fur. Total studmuffin. He had resting you-obviously-didn't-study face, which was why I called him Professor. The Studmuffin part was obvious, and I'd always liked the name Salvitore. He looked so regal and serious that I added the III at the end. His name fit him to a T.

He specialized in zero-calorie cakes that didn't pack on the pounds but tasted like they should. He also brewed the perfect cup of coffee or tea. His other skills included finding the most uncomfortable places to nap and purring as loud as the cars I worked on. He had more magic in one little murder mitten than I ever would, but I loved him fiercely. Even failed witches needed familiars, I supposed, and he was all mine.

"Oh, you're coming with me?" I scrunched my nose up at him as he trotted past toward my car.

It was after hours at Sunray's. Boxy had already gone home to his secret ninja fortress I'd been to exactly zero times. Begrudgingly, I was headed to Speedy Zone with Travis's contract so I could throw it in his face.

Studmuffin pawed at my car door and blinked expectantly at me over his shoulder.

"I'll take that as a yes," I muttered.

It made me nervous to drive with him since he insisted on sitting in my lap, paws at ten and two on the steering wheel. I'd once tried to wrestle him into a cat carrier for safety's sake before hitting the road, but it hadn't gone well. We'd stayed home instead, me nursing my wounds and Studmuffin nursing his pride. That was obviously the last time that would ever happen.

I opened the door of my muscle car for him, a purple Pontiac Firebird I named Bernadette. The feminine version of a Studmuffin. It ran like a dream because of course it did. My familiar hopped in, and soon we were cruising through the quaint, bustling streets of downtown Belle's Cove.

It was an early Friday evening in June, too hot to crack the windows and let the Georgia peach-scented air breeze through our hair. I did anyway though. People strolled down the sidewalks in front of cozy shop windows, smiling, laughing, and sometimes stopping to peer inside the shops. Others sat on benches beneath the twinkling lights stringing from one tree to the next. Belle's Cove had a magical feel about it, a unique energy unlike any place I had ever visited. I couldn't imagine living anyplace else.

Speedy Zone was still open when we arrived, its neon lights blazing and cars parked haphazardly in the large parking lot.

"No falling asleep on his boot this time, all right?" I said into the top of Studmuffin's furry head.

He pressed back into my kiss like he always did.

"Okay, but that wasn't an agreement that you won't fall asleep on his boot."

He yawned and waited for me to open the door for him. Witch, servant. Was there really a difference to him?

"Welcome, welcome!" a cheery voice said as soon as we walked in the front door.

It didn't come from the woman sitting behind the counter. She looked half crazed as if she'd heard the automatic door greeting one too many times. She looked in her early twenties, and her expertly winged eyeliner made her resemble a cat. Just...how? How do women do that so well with their makeup? Whenever I tried, I looked like a panda bear.

"We close in thirty minutes," she barked.

Ah, good old Southern hospitality. Like the woman's tone, Speedy Zone was the opposite of warm and inviting. The lights were too bright, the tile floors too polished, and there was a distinct lack of cake, coffee, and tea scents. The place stank of oil and exhaust. Not good at all.

"I'll be out in one," I told the woman. "Is Travis Black here?"

She jerked her head toward a side hallway and then peered over the counter at Studmuffin. "I don't think you can have cats in here."

"Oh, he's not a cat. He's a familiar studmuffin."

Frowning, she tilted her head. "A what?"

My familiar and I grinned, and we sauntered down the hallway past a bathroom toward a small office. Precarious stacks of file folders and loose papers were piled everywhere, on the desk, on the floor, leaving hardly any room for Travis, let alone the two of us. Without knocking, we wedged ourselves in anyway.

"Hey," I said, my voice crisp.

Behind us from the bathroom, running water and humming sounded.

"Hey. I thought I heard your spice coming." Travis stood and weaved toward us. He looked bored and tired and not at all surprised to see me, which angered me even more.

"You heard...right." Oh no. There went Studmuffin, straight to Travis's left cowboy boot again, but a different pair from last night. These were a reddish color, the toes worn and faded.

Travis smiled. "I think your cat likes me."

"He's like this with everyone." Except he wasn't at all. He tolerated most people, but there was something about Travis's boots that made him sleepy. Sleepi*er*.

Studmuffin tapped the boot as if to test its softness and then rubbed his cheek all over it. *Such* a fluffer-stinker.

"Did you roll yourself in catnip or something?" I asked Travis.

"Well, obviously." The green in his hazel eyes sparked with humor. "Is this visit work-related or did you just miss me?"

"*Miss* you?" I took a deep, steadying breath. This man was really something special if he actually thought I'd missed him. "Look, I hunted you down to let you know I'm not interested in buying Speedy Zone. Find another buyer. Or grow a pair of cement boots to sink you back to the pit you oozed from."

He lifted his eyebrows and nodded, as if agreeing with me that that might be the best choice. "How does one grow cement boots? Are there special seeds for that or...?"

I shoved the folded-up contract at his chest, my fingertips meeting hard steel underneath his black T-shirt. "You're going to drive me insane, aren't you? Did you hear a word I said? I'm not interested."

"Wait." He wrapped his hand around my wrist as I started to leave, his index finger empty of his glowing blue ring. "What are you doing tomorrow at eight o'clock?"

The question pulled me up short. What did that have to do with not buying Speedy Zone? "Why?"

"Just...hear me out." Something shifted behind his tired, shadowed eyes, as if he'd been struck by something he'd just read on my face.

"I don't owe you anything."

"No. You don't. But I have a…" He chuckled. "Pro-posal."

"Does it involve you disappearing from my life?"

He shrugged, his rough fingers still attached to my wrist. "It…could. Eventually. And I'll even promise to figure out the whole cement shoes thing and keep you posted."

I sank my eyes closed and sighed. "I'm listening."

"Come to our farm at eight o'clock for cobbler with my grandmother and me." He paused a beat, as if to gauge my reaction. "As my fiancée."

I blinked hard at him until I feared I might pull an eye muscle. Had he really just asked me that? The nerve!

"Have a nice life." I yanked my arm free and glanced down at my familiar to tell him we were leaving, but he was already sound asleep on Travis's boot.

I smacked my forehead. "You shouldn't fraternize with the enemy," I told Studmuffin.

"Wait." Travis laughed. "You won't come even for peach cobbler?"

I groaned silently. He didn't play fair. "Why could you possibly want me to pretend to be your fiancée? You didn't even know who I was at Sunray's."

"I know. You're right." He shook his head, suddenly looking even more tired than he had seconds ago. "It's been a hard year for Gran, and I said something stupid to cheer her up and…" He dragged a hand down his face as he turned back to me, and I caught a glimpse of sadness in his eyes. "Never mind. I'll handle it."

I sighed, feeling a little bit like a jerk. Just because his dad was awful didn't mean he was awful too.

"Why did your dad steal from my dad all those years ago?"

"I don't know. I would ask him, but he's dead."

Oh. I hadn't known. I started to say I was sorry, but stopped because I didn't know that I was. It sounded terrible, but it was the truth. Dad and I had been almost homeless since most of Dad's money had been tied up in the auto shop. Then, like it was carried away by a great wind, most of that money was gone.

"I'm not my dad, Victoria. I swear," Travis said, searching my face as if for a sign I could ever believe him. "All I'm trying to do is make what he did right. That's all."

He sounded so genuine, but I wasn't about to run into such a big business decision full-speed ahead. I needed to know for sure I could trust him. Even if I ever did trust him, his offer to buy Speedy Zone still felt like it scraped raw everything Dad had lost.

"So I'll see you tomorrow at eight o'clock for cobbler?" he asked hopefully.

"Nope," I said, popping the p sound, and turned to leave. "You won't. Go find another fiancée. Studmuffin, we're leaving."

My familiar perked awake and followed, leaving Travis smirking after us with his contract in his hand.

"I have a feeling I'll see you again, Victoria," he said.

I huffed. "Sounds like a threat." That man could very well be the death of me.

Back down the hallway, the sound of running water and someone humming came from a half-open door that was probably the bathroom. In the entryway, a large window behind the empty counter looked out into the garage part of the shop. Next to the window stood a closed door.

Just a peek was all I wanted. No harm done, right? A chance to study my competition up close and personal, though really it wasn't much competition at all.

I started toward the window, but Studmuffin zipped in front of me so I almost tripped over him.

"I just want to look," I whispered to him.

When I glanced down, I found him trying to turn himself into a porcupine. His fur had bristled, and his ears lay flat. He held perfectly still, his warm body pressed to my legs as if to keep me there.

"Studmuffin, can you move, please?"

Why was he freaking out? I flicked my gaze to the large garage window but didn't see anything particularly out of the ordinary. Several lines of cars sat with their hoods open. Near the back of the garage was the hydraulic lift used for changing tires or working on the bottom of cars. The lifts were raised at uneven intervals, but there was no car held aloft by them. Odd, but not exactly the stuff nightmares or kitty warnings were made of.

Shaking my head, I leaped over my familiar and ran to the door that led to the garage before he could stop me. I opened it—and then stopped. From this angle, I could see through all the opened hoods to a truck below the raised, uneven hydraulic lifts. An unmoving pair of legs poked out from right un-derneath the truck's tires.

I sucked in a shaky breath. The truck must've fall-en from the lifts. *Exactly* the stuff nightmares were made of, because whoever those legs belonged to, their owner was surely dead.

Toward the back of the garage, a streak of yellow movement blurred. Someone wearing a yellow jacket darted out the back and slammed the door behind them. Why would someone be running away, not calling 911 or telling Travis, the manager, what happened?

I started to turn to do just that when my gaze landed on the steel beams that supported the hydraulic lifts. I knew this brand of lift, had considered buying one for Sunray's, so I knew exactly where the relief valve should've been. Relief valves basically made the hydraulics work. Only there wasn't a valve. Just an empty space where one used to be, and valves didn't just fall off.

This poor person had been murdered.

I blinked down at my hand still on the doorknob, my fingerprints smudging the bronze finish. This could look really bad, me being here, what with the history between Speedy Zone and Sunray's and all.

"Oh no, Studmuffin." I gulped loudly. *"Oh no."*

Chapter Three
Detective Brawls & Disco Balls

A BELLE'S COVE POLICE detective in his mid-to-late thirties with a black button-up shirt, a tan tie and pants, and a permanent frown approached me. Studmuffin and I sat on the curb next to my car, Bernadette. Red and blue lights flashed all over Speedy Zone's parking lot. The whole place had been turned into a crime scene within minutes.

"You were the one to discover the victim, ma'am?" the detective asked.

"Yes." Numbly, I stood with my familiar in my arms, craving his comfort more than anything right now.

"Name's Detective Palmer." He flipped open a little notebook and poised a pen over it. "And yours?"

"Victoria Fox."

He scribbled that down. "Cat's name?"

"Is he a suspect?"

The detective eyed us both suspiciously.

"Professor Studmuffin Salvitore III."

Detective Palmer's frown deepened as he wrote that down as well. "You knew the victim?"

"I don't know. Who was it?"

"Jake Williams."

My shoulders slumped. "Oh. Yes, I know him. I had no idea he worked here. I went to school with him, elementary through high school. We graduated the same year."

He'd always been so nice to me and had even stuck up for me whenever I was teased while trying to read aloud. The fact that he was dead, murdered, felt like a kick to the chest.

Studmuffin swatted at the red and blue lights swirling over the detective's badge he wore next to his gun holster. I pulled him away, but he was already caught in the pretty lights' trance. His huge eyes followed their every reflection in the badge.

Detective Palmer cleared his throat, obviously irritated. "Other than the relief valve on the hydraulic system missing, did you see anything suspicious?"

I nodded, folding my hand over Studmuffin's murder mittens. "Someone was in the garage when I saw what happened, but they left out the back."

"Did you get a good look at them?"

"They were wearing a yellow jacket, but the rest of them was a blur."

The detective made a note of that in his notepad. "What were you talking to Travis about?"

Studmuffin flashed both paws out from underneath my hand to catch the lights in the detective's badge. He even made a clicking sound in the back of his throat as he *tap, tap, tapped* the lights.

"Now is not the time for hunting," I scolded and pulled him away again. "Travis wants me to buy this shop from him, when really, it should belong to my dad. Travis's dad, Marcus Black, and my dad used to be business partners before Marcus took the money and ran. I gave Travis back his contract unsigned."

"So Sunray's is now your shop?"

"Mine and Boxy's, yes."

"Did you argue with Travis?"

"Well...yes. That's the only way to communicate with him. He's impossible." I said it like it was obvious, which earned me a sharp look from Detective Palmer.

Yep, this was going *so* well.

"How's business at Sunray's, Ms. Fox?"

"It's great. Never better."

"Did you come here to cause harm to Speedy Zone's business?"

My jaw dropped. "Of course not."

"Did you kill Jake Williams?"

Studmuffin chose that moment to dive-bomb the detective's badge face-first, fangs out, claws out, *all* the things out.

"No! Stop that!" He was in such a frenzy that it took all my muscles to wrestle him away. "I'm sorry. It's the lights on your badge," I explained. "He thinks it's a disco ball and that it must be destroyed."

Detective Palmer waited for my answer as though my familiar hadn't just attacked him. His gunmetal-gray eyes remained locked on me, unflinching in their seriousness. Broody detective was broody.

"I wouldn't dream of killing anyone, especially Jake Williams," I said.

"But you did argue with Travis. Were you still angry when you left him?"

Just his existence made me angry, which was why I'd told him to grow cement boots. Had Travis told Detective Palmer that? Today really hadn't shone the best light on me. I should've stayed home, counted Studmuffin's dots on his tummy, anything but this.

I sighed. "Travis asked me to be his fiancée."

The detective's eyebrows sprang up his forehead, his first show of emotion...ever, probably. "He asked you to marry him?"

"No. He asked me to pretend to be his fiancée for the sake of his grandmother. So yes, I was angry about that. It's a rather strange thing to ask someone."

Detective Palmer wrote for a long time in his notebook. He turned his body away from the pretty lights, much to Studmuffin's disappointment.

My familiar crossed his paws over my arm innocently and tossed me a glare as though I'd just crushed his disco-ball dreams. I rolled my eyes at him.

"Why did you enter the garage?" the detective finally asked.

"I just wanted a peek."

He gave me a knowing stare. "At the competition."

"Well, yes," I admitted. "Look, if I did kill Jake, do you really think I'd be sticking around here afterward?"

He blinked at me expectantly.

"The answer is no, I wouldn't, and no, I didn't kill him." Honestly, if he thought I was lying, why wasn't he arresting me already?

He fixed me with his steely gaze. "But you do have a motive, Ms. Fox, and you were at the scene of the crime. There's no denying that."

"Did you dust for prints on the hydraulic lift yet?" I blurted.

"Are you telling me how to do my job?" he fired back.

I forced a smile that probably made me look like I forgot to pay my brain bill. "Yes?"

"Please don't," he said, his tone crisp. "Also, please don't refer to my badge as a disco ball again."

"Right." I grimaced. "Sorry."

"You're free to go, but I wouldn't leave Belle's Cove if I were you, Ms. Fox." He turned and strode away, his footsteps abrupt and no-nonsense, just like the rest of him.

"Wasn't planning on it," I muttered and plunked down on the sidewalk again with Studmuffin. My thoughts were too heavy to drive home just yet, and my mouth had probably made everything ten times worse. "What have I gotten myself into?"

My familiar whipped his head around at the sound of approaching footsteps made by his favorite pair of boots. He sprang out of my arms toward Travis and flanked his legs like they'd known each other forever.

"Traitor," I grumbled.

Travis bent to scratch him between the ears. "Quite a day, huh?"

"Yeah."

He sank down next to me, his broad shoulder touching mine. I was too deflated to pull away, or to scold Studmuffin for flopping lazily over Travis's left boot, belly up and paws in the air.

"I went to school with Jake," I said. "Real nice guy. I can't imagine anyone wanting to kill him."

"He was my best employee. He was always on time and worked hard." Sighing, Travis stroked

Studmuffin's belly. "He did sometimes talk about a crazy girlfriend though."

I nodded, my mind already spinning about who could've done it. "The lady with the great eyeliner behind the counter... Where did she go?"

"In my office bawling her eyes out. She was getting ready to mop and didn't hear a thing over the water filling the bucket."

"Mopping an already clean floor?"

Travis shrugged. "I have her do it three times a day between greeting customers."

"Greeting might be an exaggeration," I muttered, but I wasn't sure he heard me.

He glanced up from melting my familiar further over his boot. "You don't approve of mopping?"

"Three times a day is excessive when I'm sure she can help in other ways." I sighed, suddenly exhausted. "You said yourself my shop is filthy. That's because Boxy and I don't spend all our time cleaning. We fix the cars, Studmuffin feeds the customers, and they go home happy."

Travis stopped his rubbing and slowly turned to look at me, his mouth slightly open. "I get what you're saying, but on the other hand I don't have a clue what you're saying. Studmuffin feeds your customers? Your *cat*?"

Oops. I hadn't spilled that secret to anyone before, but Detective Palmer had put me in a nothing-but-the-truth mood. Customers just assumed I made the cakes, spiced the teas, brewed the coffee, *and* fixed the cars. It was easier to let them think that. Much easier than explaining why my cat did magic, and I did not.

Travis was blinking at me expectantly. Too late to gobble back my words now. Besides, lying to him after I'd become suspect number one in a murder case probably would only make me look like I had something to hide.

"He's my familiar," I admitted. "And I'm—"

"A witch." He whistled low, which made Studmuffin knead the air in his sleep for some reason. Travis stared at me but not like I'd grown a wart on my nose. More like he wasn't quite sure if he should run away from the big, bad witch or not. Actually, it was the exact same expression either way.

"Relax," I told him. "I don't use my magic for evil." Or for good. Or for any reason.

"I see..." He gazed out across the parking lot to the crime scene tape flapping in a light breeze. "Which coven are you in?"

"I'm...between covens at the moment." Sure, that sounded legit. The truth was I never had a coven. It would've been great to have that magical support group growing up to help me read the spells from my grimoire correctly. Keyword—correctly. A single misread word, and I'd destroyed half a city block and nearly took down Sunray's with it. That happened in high school, seventeen years ago. I never admitted to Dad what happened. Afterward, I never cracked open my grimoire again.

I glanced at the deep frown on Travis's face and slumped my shoulders farther. "Now that you know my secret, you think I killed Jake with my witchy powers, don't you?"

"The thought crossed my mind," he admitted.

Awesome. Let this day live in history as the absolute worst.

"But why would you point out that the hydraulic valve was missing if you killed him? Why would you admit to me of all people that you're a witch right after?" He bumped my shoulder with his gently. "You're not stupid, Victoria. You're not a murderer, either."

Unexpected warmth blossomed up my neck to my cheeks. "Yes," I cried. "Finally someone who's making sense."

"Careful," he said with a chuckle. "That sounded an awful lot like a compliment."

"Don't get your hopes up."

"Come meet my grandma tomorrow night," he said, his voice softer. "She knows all about witches and that kind of thing. She might be able to recommend a coven for you."

I heaved a lengthy sigh. "I'm not going as your fiancée."

"I'll tell her the truth. Promise." He smiled down at Studmuffin's toe beans sticking up in the air. "You're just a long-time friend of the Black family who likes peach cobbler, and nothing more. She'll be delighted to see you again, I'm sure."

I wasn't a friend, though, was I? Of Travis Black, son of Marcus Black who'd nearly made Sunray's nonexistent? Then again, I'd also nearly made the shop nonexistent because of my dyslexia when I blew up half the city block. If Grandma Black could help somehow, I had to go. Besides, if I was seen with Travis, maybe it would help clear my name of Jake's murder and prove I didn't want to harm Speedy Zone. That could just as easily backfire, but still, peach cobbler. That pretty much settled it.

"Eight o'clock?" I asked.

"Eight o'clock." Travis grinned. "Can I see your phone? I'll give you my number in case you get lost."

I snorted. "I don't get lost."

"In case *I* get lost, then.

That didn't even make sense, but I handed over my phone anyway.

Once he'd put his number into my cell, he said, "So on a scale of one to ten, one being never and ten as definitely, what did you think the chances were of getting questioned for murder today?"

"With you in the picture?" Taking back my phone, I rose and dusted off my backside. "At least an eight."

Chapter Four

The Delicate Unboxing of Ninja Boxy Part One

WHEN DAD SPOKE OF Boxy, he'd lovingly refer to him as "brother," air quotes included. Not necessarily *his* "brother" though. I never knew if that made Boxy my "uncle" or not, or if he really was a ninja like both he and Dad often hinted. He was a true man of mystery.

I did know one thing though. Two things, actually. I couldn't run Sunray's without him, and I loved my "uncle ninja" with my whole heart.

"Vic!" While standing on a step ladder, he bent double over the hood of Ms. Stevenson's massive bookmobile parked in the shop's garage. "There's something really wrong here."

"What?" I glanced behind me, clipboard in hand. I was mid-inventory which didn't take a lot of time for me because I had the item order on the sheet memorized.

"I don't think I have the know-how to fix it."

I chuckled. "I don't believe you."

Boxy grabbed his cane where he'd left it on the bumper and stepped down from the ladder. "I better go break the news to poor Ms. Stevenson."

"Tell me what's wrong with it. The suspense is killing me," I said, moving toward him.

Sighing heavily, he whipped off his blue-and-white striped railroad cap and mopped his face with it. When he took it away, he revealed his sly grin. "The beast is out of gas."

I mock gasped. "Whatever will we do?"

"I'm thinking we top off all her fluids, including the gas, and do an inspection, all free of charge. Crazy, right?"

"Your brand of crazy is my favorite." I nudged him with my shoulder. "I'll start on it while you call your girlfr— I mean our best bookmobile customer."

Boxy wagged his finger at me, his one eye twinkling as bright as any star and his grin beaming. "You don't know nothing about nothing, little Vic."

"Uh-huh." I clicked my tongue. "Then why are you blushing?"

"It's hot. It's Georgia." He shrugged and tripped away from me, a very unBoxy-like thing to do. Even with his cane, he was more spry and graceful than most people in their sixties. Maybe even their twenties. "It's Georgia hot."

A sudden realization widened my eyes, and a little ball of giddiness bounced throughout my stomach.

"You're in love with her," I whisper-shouted. "Since when?"

"Since nope." His blush deepened all the way to the tips of his ears poking out of his cap. Tilting his head, he scurried to the waiting area. "I do believe I hear the phone ringing."

I pointed to the phone hanging on the wall above the trash can. "It's really not."

"But it could from the one inside."

Laughing, I let him go. Poor guy had it bad, and I'd never known. He was never one to open up to me about much of anything, which was fine. I enjoyed figuring things out on my own, and I did know enough about him already to read him well. Ms. Stevenson had spun him about big time. I wanted details for no other reason than I needed something else to think about other than Jake's murder and tonight's...whatever with Travis Black's gran. *Anything* other than those things. But first, I wanted to fix the bookmobile. No thought required since it was automatic.

I snorted. Bad car humor was my favorite.

"Meow," Studmuffin said from on top of the bookmobile. He gazed down on me while standing on his back legs with his white chest puffed out. This was what I called his power pose, which was just another way for him to demand to be worshipped.

"Yes, yes. All hail the king." I swept low into a dramatic bow. "Thank you for gracing me, a lowly human, with your presence. You are the greatest familiar who has ever lived."

He slow-blinked at me as if those were the words he'd been waiting to hear for an eternity. Actually it had only been a few hours since I last told him that. Finding the highest perch in the garage and demanding praise was yet another hobby of his. Such a busy, hectic life.

Sort of like it usually was around here on Saturdays. Not today, even though our appointment book was packed. Weird.

Through the open garage, I spied two women younger than me walking down the sidewalk whispering and pointing. As soon as I saw them, they sprinted off like their heels had caught fire. A sinking feeling settled into my gut, but I ignored it.

While I fixed up the bookmobile, Ms. Stevenson arrived and made herself at home in the cozy little waiting area off the garage. Half a slice of ginger layer cake with poached pears and cream cheese frosting sat on her plate while she leaned back in her chair, eyes closed, a blissful smile on her face. A woman in her late fifties, she always wore bright red lipstick, now flecked with a few crumbs she ignored. She'd swept her sunshine-yellow hair up into a loose bun and dressed casually in a pretty flower top, light blue capris, and sensible loafers.

"Hi, Ms. Stevenson," I said, a little shyly, as I entered the waiting area.

When I was younger, she used to work inside Belle's Cove Public Library, not the bookmobile. She was the reason I found magic in audiobooks. She used to listen with me sometimes with the same print book open in front of me so I could follow along as the words were spoken. Afterward, we'd talk about the stories, and she'd encourage me to check out more. She was the reason I owned so many audiobooks now, the CD kind in plastic cases. I was old-school because I liked physical things like that, not digital. The CD cases were lined up alphabetically by author behind me on the wall shelves I built and painted myself. Bright blue and yellow like the first sunrays across the morning sky.

Ms. Stevenson was also the reason I considered myself a book witch, dyslexia and all, though I'd never told her that. While some witches found their magic elsewhere like in mixing potions or the earth itself, books were where I found mine. My grimoire specifically, but I found little bits of magic in almost all books.

Her eyes popped open wide, a sparkling shade of clear blue, and she wiped away the crumbs. "Lovely to see you, Victoria." She held up her plate. "Did you make this? I would love the recipe."

"I'll...see what I can do." There was no sharing of my familiar's recipes. Ever. He didn't have any since he baked by magic, and even if he did, he wasn't the sharing type. "The bookmobile is all yours when you're ready, but feel free to have another slice of ginger cake."

"No, no, I couldn't."

"It's calorie-free..." I told her in a sing-song voice.

Her jaw dropped. "There's no way!"

Boxy strolled in from the garage then, even though he hadn't been in there ten seconds ago. That wasn't what made me do a double-take though; Boxy had changed. A lot. He'd ridded himself of the railroad cap and overalls and now wore a crisp white button-down tucked into black dress pants. He'd slicked his silver hair over the bald spot the cap usually covered, and he'd traded his everyday cane for the silver and gold-scaled dragon head one. He even wore spicy cologne.

I whistled. "Dapper Boxy is dapper. Well done."

Ignoring me, Boxy caned his way to Ms. Stevenson with a shy smile on his face. "Good to see you, Isabella."

"Good to see you too. Thank you for not making me feel embarrassed about running out of gas. I get so focused on the books and all the ways I can get them into people's hands that sometimes the little stuff leaks out." She tapped her temple and shook her head. "And then the little stuff turns into big stuff, and I'm left stranded on the side of the road. What's worse is that this isn't the first time it's happened. Far from it."

"No worries." Boxy sat next to her at the little round table and patted her shoulder. "I'm just glad I could help."

Studmuffin wound his sleek body around her ankles for further consolation.

"The tow truck service offered to take the bookmobile to Speedy Zone since it was right there," Ms. Stevenson continued, "but I'm so thankful I called you, Boxy, and you said for them to take it here. If I'd taken it there, it wouldn't have been finished for this afternoon because the whole place is a crime scene now."

Studmuffin and I shared a look. Not Boxy though. Pretty sure he'd long forgotten our existence with Ms. Stevenson next to him.

"Yes, well, the problem was too complex for Speedy Zone," he said.

She frowned. "An empty gas tank?"

"Bunch of hornets in their fingers over at that place." He jazzed his fingers to help illustrate. "They break while trying to fix. We just fix."

Ms. Stevenson beamed at him. "Thank goodness."

I shifted on my feet, not wanting to ruin their moment but too curious to keep quiet. "Did you see anything strange outside Speedy Zone last night when the bookmobile broke down?"

"Strange how?" She picked up her glass of sweet tea, the ice cubes tinkling gently.

"Well..." I sighed, not sure how else to say it but to say it. "Strange like someone who'd just committed a murder. I saw someone fly out the back door of Speedy Zone last night, and the back door led to the street your poor bookmobile died on."

"Hmm, now that you mention it, while I was calling a tow truck, I did see someone fly out the back of Speedy Zone." She sipped her tea, drawing out the suspense. "Someone wearing yellow. They ran across the street in the other direction, but I couldn't tell you anything else about them."

Boxy's eyes widened, never once straying from Ms. Stevenson. "Good thing you're sitting down, Vic."

I snorted and shook my head. "I'm not."

I'd told him the exact same thing that she'd seen, and while I knew he never doubted me, it was nice to know I hadn't been hallucinating. Always a good day to hear my brain still held intact, even with all the calorie-free cake I consumed. Sometimes I was convinced that all that sugar poked holes in my brain, but then I forgot to care because cake.

"Anything else?" I prompted my favorite librarian.

She nodded as she set her sweet tea down. "Yes, there was someone else there too."

"Someone *else*?" I leaned forward. So did Boxy and Studmuffin who blinked up at her expectantly. "Who?"

"Just a shadow in a car behind Speedy Zone," she said with a shrug. "As soon as the person wearing yellow left, they sped away."

"What kind of car?" Boxy asked. "Color? Make? Model? Year?"

Ms. Stevenson stared at him blankly. "It was a car. It might've been white or yellow...or maybe tan. It had doors on it. Four, I think."

I cupped my hand over my fake cough to hide my wince, but I realized not everyone spoke car. Still, the one she saw could be one of hundreds of thousands.

"That helps. You *really* narrowed it down." Boxy patted her shoulder again, not an ounce of sarcasm on his face.

Ms. Stevenson smiled gratefully at him.

"It's a start," I agreed. "A yellow jacket is kind of an odd color choice to wear to a murder, you know?"

"My thoughts exactly," Boxy said. "This was a crime of passion, something unplanned."

"Eh..." I teetered my hand back and forth in the air in a so-so, we're-both-right gesture. "But also sort of planned if two people showed up outside the back door. That's not typically how normal, innocent people act right before a murder."

Ms. Stevenson nodded. "I'll call Detective Palmer with what I saw. I didn't think much of it, but now... Sounds like we have a real mystery on our hands. The who-done-its are the bookmobile's hottest section by far. Sometimes people thumb to the end to see who did it and why. If you ask me, those people are the real criminals, same as those who eat Cheetos while flipping pages. No need to try to convince me I'm wrong"—she jabbed her finger at the air—"because *you will fail.*"

"We wouldn't dream of it," Boxy said with a chuckle.

Ms. Stevenson relaxed into her chair again with another sip of sweet tea. "Maybe it's best to stick to one disaster at a time. Like the murder mystery we've gotten ourselves wrapped up into."

True. The other mystery was why Sunray's was so dead on a Saturday, even when Speedy Zone was closed.

Deep down, I knew. I just couldn't bear to think it.

The whispers, the looks, no one showing up for their appointments... Belle's Cove thought I committed a murder.

In the words of the great Ms. Stevenson from about ten seconds ago: *No need to try to convince me I'm wrong because you will fail.*

I just hoped I didn't fail Sunray's.

Chapter Five

Betrayed By The Sock Drawer

INSTEAD OF GOING TO Travis Black's farm, I sat on the floor in my apartment thinking about going to Travis Black's farm. My apartment was located above Sunray's, with two staircases leading up to a private entrance. One staircase was outside, and the other started in Sunray's waiting area.

There was plenty of seating in the apartment, but Studmuffin hogged the window seat while charging up his solar power. He lay so he showed off his belly, and my job was to count the black spots there before he swatted my hand. This was a game we always played with an audiobook playing in the background, but the challenge was he made his spots move. Fast. So fast I lost count within seconds.

He swatted my hand lightly, his whiskers gleaming in the sunshine over a victorious kitty smile.

"You win." I said, holding my head while the room spun around me. "Again."

See, this was what I'd much rather be doing on a Saturday evening—getting dizzy while listening to a scary, ghosty audiobook, not visiting the family of the man who wronged Dad and me.

But they're not him, a little voice in the back of my mind said. They weren't Marcus Black.

Groaning, I slumped headfirst into the window seat cushion, and the remote to my stereo which turned off the audiobook. My familiar used that opportunity to prop one leg against my forehead so he could bathe his belly spots. They'd gone still, unlike the big yellow one outside the window that slowly dipped toward twilight.

"He's not his dad, Studmuffin," I told him. "He doesn't think I'm a murderer, and he listened to me last night without judgement. He was genuinely shaken by Jake's murder, so he has real, human emotions. A plus in my book."

My cat shifted so his foreleg braced against my nose and mouth as though trying to silence me.

"Are you telling me to shush?" I moved his leg to my cheek, but he slid it right back. He knew as well as I did, though, that I'd keep talking until I was dead. Maybe even after that. "It'll be awkward if I go over there. They'll want to talk about what happened between Marcus and Dad, maybe even defend him."

Studmuffin looked at me and sighed then went back to cleaning the same spot.

"On the other hand, Travis said his gran knows all about witches. Maybe she can help me somehow. Maybe if I'm seen going to his farm, the farm of my mortal enemy, and no one ends up dead, that will help me and Sunray's." I fell silent, thinking about my beloved shop downstairs. "That's a risk I'm willing to take."

I stood, my mind made up, but my nerves cinched themselves into knots anyway.

My familiar stared up at me with wide, yellow-green eyes, the foot he'd propped on my face stuck in the air.

"I have to go," I told him, striding to the door. "Are you staying?"

He folded himself into a kitty loaf and watched me expectantly.

"Okay, you hold down the fort." I hooked my shaky fingers through the strap of my purse on a little side table next to the door. "And wish me luck."

As soon as I opened the door, a magical spark danced down my spine and steeped the air with the scent of melted chocolate. The power of it sucked the air from my lungs.

I whirled. "You wished me luck?"

The kitty loaf had never done that before. I hadn't ever asked him to though. Never needed to before now. He lay there with a rare smile, his gorgeous fur gleaming in the setting sun.

"I see what you're doing, Professor Studmuffin Salvitore III. You're making me fall in love with you all over again." As I left, I blew him a kiss and winked.

He winked right back like a proper studmuffin.

THE TWO-STORY FARMHOUSE ROSE up in the distance on a little hill, surrounded by a grove of trees with peaches weighing the limbs. The house had been painted slate gray a long time ago, but the paint had peeled to a yucky brown. Shutters hung at weird angles, and a dead garden surrounded the wide front porch. The whole place looked like something from a *Sleepy Hollow* movie set. The spooky part of me loved it. The practical part of me wondered what had happened. It had been so long since I'd last been here, but I knew it had never looked like this before.

With my stomach in knots, I parked in the U-shaped drive in front of the house. What was I getting myself into? I hated awkward situations and awkward conversations and awkward everything. I'd rather dig myself a hole and live there. This felt awfully similar to being forced to read aloud in elementary school.

But this wasn't then. It was now, and it was my responsibility to clear my name of a murder I didn't commit. If I didn't, Sunray's might not survive.

Taking a deep breath that did absolutely nothing to calm me, I clambered out of Bernadette and marched to the porch. Voices carried from inside the house through the not-quite-closed front door.

"Ow!"

"You better believe ow!"

That was Travis's voice and probably his gran's. I peered through the crack in the door, raising my hand to knock, but the sight in front of me stalled my brain. First, the inside of the house hadn't been neglected like the outside. The wooden floors had been polished to a high shine, and the scent of fresh-brewed peach tea wafted out. Second, a little old woman dressed head-to-toe in a peach velour sweat suit with the word Juicy written across the shirt stood in the hallway. She faced off with Travis holding a Ping-Pong paddle in front of her, wielding it like a light saber. And third, she had a glowing blue ring exactly like Travis's.

"Gran, whoa!" Travis said, backing away from her. "What did I do now?"

"More like what you *didn't* do," she shrieked.

Quick as a lightning bug's wink, she whacked him on the backside with her paddle.

"Okay..." He held his hands up to ward her off. "Did two spanks cover it or is there more?"

"I'm not sure yet," she shot back, wrinkling her nose. "Now, I am silently judging you."

"I'm suddenly doubting every life decision I've ever made," he said.

Me too. And I was just the eavesdropper. I'd never seen a grown man shrink in size with the power of his grandma's glare.

"Well, you better. Because look what I found." Grandma Black held up a ring. "I thought you put a ring on it, so imagine my surprise when I was putting your socks away and found it hidden in a place you didn't want me to find. Guess what?" With her ring hand, she yanked her sweatpants up and snapped the waistband in place, the sound just as sharp as her voice. "I found it. But I don't see a woman's finger attached to it, which I suppose is a good thing in and of itself because at least you're not a collector of body parts"—she held up a finger—"*that I know of*. You told me you gave it to Felicia, asked her to marry you, and that it was a done deal. Set in stone. *This* stone."

"Gran, I can explain—"

She put her hand with the Ping-Pong paddle on her hip. "I did not find Felicia in your sock drawer, Travis, and I need you to tell me why."

He sighed. "Of all the things I expected to hear today, none of them involved Felicia in my sock drawer. She's in Duluth."

Gran narrowed her hazel eyes. "Are you still planning on marrying her?"

Sighing, Travis placed his hands on his hips. "No, Gran. I wanted to tell you, but I didn't want to upset you."

"Did she want a different ring or something, and you didn't tell me because you thought it would hurt my feelings?" Her eyes filled with tears, and my heart broke for her.

"No, it just didn't work out between us." Travis seemed to whither as he watched her face crumple. Immediately, he wrapped her up in a big hug, letting her soak her tears into his shirt.

"Then who's coming for cobbler if it isn't Felicia?" she asked between sniffles.

"A friend. Victoria. Remember her?"

Was I a friend, though? I didn't think so, especially since I was standing here like a creeper.

"I was going to tell you the truth before she got here," Travis continued, "but my sock drawer gave me away."

"I just want you to be happy with someone, Travis, for you to find your person. It's reason enough to start drinking straight from the whiskey bottle," she said.

He laughed and squeezed her harder. "When did you ever stop?"

She whacked him again on the backside with her lethal Ping-Pong paddle. He groaned. He probably wouldn't be able to sit for a week, and he deserved it. I stifled a laugh, or tried to anyway.

Both their heads swiveled my way.

Travis grinned, genuine surprise on his face. "You came."

"Um, hi. The door was open. I only just got here two seconds ago." Totally didn't overhear a very personal conversation from start to finish. *Nope.*

Grandma Black waved me inside. "Well, don't be a stranger. Victoria, you say? Why do I feel like I know that name?" She patted her wet cheeks. "Look at me! I must look a fright."

"You look just fine, Mrs. Black," I assured her. Then with a deep, steadying breath, I entered the Black family home for the first time in...I don't even know how long.

Chapter Six

Something Wasn't There When the Candle Burned

THE BLACKS' FARMHOUSE WAS cozy yet modern, lived in but clean, with exposed boards crisscrossing over the high ceilings that matched the polished grain of the floors below. What looked like handmade quilts lay draped over the two couches in the living room. The flat-screen TV against one wall showed wavy lines over what looked like a recording of a really old soap opera.

"Please, call me Gran," Grandma Black said. "Everyone else does. Can I get you some peach iced tea, sugar?"

Travis leaned closer to my ear and whispered, "The correct answer is yes."

"Yes. Please." I smiled politely. I remembered her vaguely from when Dad and I visited when I was super young, but I wasn't so sure she remembered me.

"Victoria...Victoria." She gasped, her whole face frozen in shock. "Oh! Victoria Fox, it's *you*. My goodness, sugar, you have grown into a beautiful young lady. How long has it been?"

"Um, a while."

A hint of devastation passed behind her eyes, but she covered it up with a smile. She gestured left down another hallway decorated with all sizes of framed photos. "Have a seat in the dining room, and we'll have cobbler for our very special guest. We didn't have dinner, and I'm starving." She fluttered through a doorway into what I thought was the kitchen, quick and spry as a bird.

"Ladies first." Travis held out his arm for me to precede him down the hall.

As I did, I avoided looking too closely at the hanging photos in case I saw one of Marcus. "You have dessert as supper, too, I see."

"In this house, dessert is the only food group that matters," Travis said, following behind. "That, and peach tea."

I nodded as we entered the dining room, most of which was taken up by the massive oak table built for six. "Dessert is at the bottom of the food pyramid for a reason—to support the other, smaller food groups."

Travis chuckled as he pulled out an ornate, high-backed chair for me. "I don't know which food pyramid you've been looking at, but I like your version much better. You, uh, heard all of that out on the porch?"

"I did," I admitted while I sat.

Travis sighed, sinking down in the chair next to me. "I can hear her sometimes crying in her room at night. Other than me, she's alone, and she doesn't want that for me. I get it, which is why about a week or so ago I felt my mouth moving before my foggy, tired brain could react and stuff my mouth with *other* words. Better words. Not those words, which were 'Felicia's coming over to meet you. She's my brand new fiancée.'" He propped his elbows on the table and scrubbed his eyes. "We broke up shortly before that. I hate lying to my gran. I hate disappointing her even more. And now I've done both."

It was kind of odd seeing someone in the Black family feel guilt and love so openly. Marcus hadn't, at least to my knowledge. Honestly, it was a little refreshing. It made this family more complicated than I'd once thought, realer somehow, flaws and all.

"So don't lie to her again," I said simply.

Travis snorted a laugh and sat back in his seat. "Believe me, I won't. But I appreciate the blunt advice." He looked at me closely. "You sure do say what you mean, don't you?"

"Always." My gaze caught on the dark circles under his eyes, seemingly a permanent fixture to his face. "You mentioned you were tired and foggy. Why is that?"

He jerked his thumb toward a side window. "Those peach trees outside? They're priority number one since they're Gran's main source of income, with the rest of the farm coming in at number two. Speedy Zone is so far down my priority list that it's barely hanging on."

"So that's why you want to sell it."

He nodded. "Everyone who's offered to buy Speedy Zone before now has seemed to suddenly remember they have to pay for their kid's braces when they don't even have kids."

"Funny how that works."

An awkward silence fell over the table then, all because he'd brought up Speedy Zone. Just the name gave me the chilly willies since it had no warmth or depth. Sunray's had both. It was named after my dad, Ray, and his nickname for me, Sunray.

Luckily Gran hurried in to save the day, somehow balancing three peach iced teas, a fresh pan of peach cobbler, a pint of vanilla ice cream, bowls, spoons, napkins, and her Ping-Pong paddle. "Here we are," she said, enunciating each word. "Still warm, so dig in a la mode or without."

Travis leaped up from the table. "Here, let me help."

"*Get*." While carrying all of that, she somehow managed to swat at him like a pesky fly with her paddle.

I laughed. So did Travis.

When she set the cobbler and tea in the center of the table, my mouth watered, and I wasn't even hungry.

"I brought extra spoons in case you need one for each hand," Gran said, settling herself across from us. "I know I do."

"Smart," I said, taking another spoon to humor her.

"Isn't it though?" She winked at Travis, who shook his head and laughed.

Once we were all served, I took a spoonful in, and perfectly baked peaches with a flaky, buttery crust melted over my tongue. Absolute heaven. Studmuffin might have some competition with Gran. Too bad cat versus human bake-offs weren't a real thing.

"Victoria, I sure do miss your dad. He practically lived here growing up, you know. He used to call me his adopted mom and give me a run for my money at Ping-Pong before…" She stared into space toward another time, her spoons of cobbler temporarily forgotten in midair. Then she shook herself out of her reverie. "Is he doing well?"

"He's doing just fine. Last I heard from him, he was in Melbourne, Australia. He was talking so fast about his and Chloe's honeymoon adventures there, all I heard mention of was opera kangaroos."

Gran laughed, a deep belly one that made me smile. "I'm glad. He deserves it, though I do wish he would've invited me to his and Chloe's wedding."

"Gran," Travis said gently. "Maybe now's not the time."

"Of course it's time," she said matter-of-factly. "Part of the Fox family is here. That means the rift between all of us isn't as wide and deep and hurtful as I imagined. Marcus loved your dad, Victoria. I think his broken heart about what he did is what did him in. I am not excusing his actions. Not one single bit. All I'm saying is that seeing you again is a breath of fresh air."

"Thank you." I bowed my head, my cheeks flushing, unsure what to say next because I didn't really want to talk about it. What was done was done, and these two people didn't have anything to do with what Marcus did to Dad. I was beginning to see that now. "I… I will admit that me coming here was a little bit for selfish reasons."

Gran swallowed a huge bite of cobbler. "Oh, how so?"

"People think she killed Jake as part of a plot to watch Speedy Zone go down in flames." Travis turned to me with a knowing smile. "She's trying to make nice and mend the rift."

My jaw dropped into my lap. Wow. Way to read me like an open book. Had I been that obvious?

"It's what I would do if our roles were reversed." He shrugged. "She's also here for the cobbler, tea, and good company of course."

I stared at him in disbelief. "Do I get to talk now? Or are you going to start finishing my—"

"Sentences?" He grinned, a lopsided one that had no business looking so good on his face. "Do you want me t—"

"*No*," I said, ignoring all my Southern manners. "You should have more cobbler so you're quiet for five glorious seconds."

"Can't." He leaned back and patted his flat stomach. "No more room."

"Don't be disgusting." Gran swatted him lightly on the elbow. "No one has just one piece. Get on in there for another so Victoria and I can enjoy five glorious seconds of girl talk."

"You'll have to roll me upstairs," As if she'd twisted his arm, he reluctantly picked up the serving spatula and started to slice more cobbler from the center.

Well, I use slice loosely. More like maim.

Gran looked on in horror. "I will roll you out of this house if you don't stop that. Why are you stabbing the cobbler to death? Give me that."

She plucked the spatula from his fingers and salvaged his piece with a nice, neat cut. She placed the piece on his plate. With a wink at me, she said, "Those five glorious seconds of silence start now."

Chuckling, Travis tried to find all the hidden places inside of him that weren't full of hot air to stuff more cobbler. He gazed at me expectantly, those twinkling hazel eyes of his daring me to share more of my secrets before he did. Yet somehow, I think even he knew this one was mine and mine alone to share.

"The other reason I'm here is because I'm a witch," I blurted before I lost my nerve.

Gran gasped and clutched the edge of the table. "A witch? How long have you known?"

"Well, since my mom left me a grimoire and magic sparked out of my fingertips as soon as I touched it."

"Oh, dear Victoria, you poor thing." She patted the place over her heart and shook her head with a pained smile. "A witch growing up without a mother. You must've been so lost. I'm so sorry."

I nodded, never quite sure what to say when people talked about my mom. She left soon after I was born.

"Did you find a coven to help you?" Gran asked.

"Not yet. Are there any covens in Belle's Cove?"

"Sure there are. There's lots." Gran smiled kindly, without any judgement that I probably should already have a coven since I was the ripe old age of thirty-five. "I can help you find the perfect one for you if you'd like."

"Thank you. I'd appreciate it." At the thought of joining a coven, my stomach flipped sideways, so I immediately stuffed my mouth with more cobbler to give my stomach more weight and to slow it down.

There was a reason my grimoire lay on top of The Place To Put Things I Don't Want To Think About Today. If I joined a coven, I'd have to address my dyslexia in front of strangers. On the other hand, if they were the right coven, maybe it wouldn't be so bad. Besides, just tonight I'd done something I never thought I'd do. Last night, too, when I'd stumbled into a murder and became a suspect. This was becoming a week of firsts, and my nerves weren't exactly thrilled about it.

"The first coven that comes to mind is the AGs," Gran said.

"The Attorney Generals?" Travis asked.

Gran rolled her eyes at him. "The Anything Goes coven. They accept witches of all skill levels and are known to be very open-minded."

"Well, I'm definitely a beginner," I said. "How do you know so much about witches?"

"Oh, no reason." Gran yanked her ring hand from the tabletop and settled it into her lap as though I hadn't already seen it. "I've just lived in this town long enough to know all sorts of things. That's all."

Travis also had his ring hand hidden underneath the table, his mouth firmly sealed closed. What were they being so secretive about? Were their rings crafted by a secret coven? Were they witches themselves? If they were witches, too, why not just tell me since I'd told them? Only it seemed quite a bit more complicated than that. Call it intuition or a sixth sense or a strange itch on the back of my neck, but I didn't think they were witches. There was something else going on with them. Something they didn't want me to know.

They were probably aliens.

"More cobbler?" Gran offered, already slicing another piece. Her voice pitched higher into an unnatural squeak.

Definitely aliens, but I wouldn't mind being body snatched if I had more cobbler first.

"You bet." I shoved my empty plate closer.

"Thatta girl," she said. "This'll help to keep you from blowing away. We used to count our calories around here, but we lost count."

"If you eat after sundown, it's too dark to see the calories." Travis also scooted his empty plate closer for another piece. "Therefore, they don't exist."

A slow smile crept over Gran's face as she gazed across the table at him. "I knew I liked you for a reason. I think I'll keep you."

Travis grinned. "So you'll put the Ping-Pong paddle away, then?"

"Not on your life," she told him.

I chuckled. I liked these two together. They obviously loved each other. I liked Travis's warmth and humor around Gran too.

It must've been all the sugar eating holes into my brain, but I couldn't deny he was easy on the eyes. He looked relaxed, at home, and better suited for farm life than behind his chaotic desk at Speedy Zone.

He turned and caught me looking. I pretended I was looking for my second spoon while my ears flushed hot.

"Mm-*hmm*," Gran murmured into her tea glass as she took a drink.

I could feel her doing a squinty eye thing between the two of us. I could also feel Travis's gaze. He didn't bother to look away.

"When will you open Speedy Zone again?" I asked, carefully cutting off a bite of cobbler with my spoon.

He cleared his throat. "Monday morning. It will be so strange going back there. My employees are nervous. They think the place is cursed with bad luck now."

Gran reached across the table and patted his hand. "Understandable. That's a hard thing to have to deal with, especially while still dealing with the shock of Jake's murder. Such a tragedy."

Travis sighed. "I just don't understand why someone would want him dead. He was such a likeable guy. Always friendly. Never a harsh word for anyone."

"You're sure about that?" Gran raised a skeptical eyebrow.

"Well, yeah." Travis frowned. "I worked with him every day."

"Why?" I leaned forward, my spoonful hovering near my mouth forgotten. "Do you know something about Jake?"

Gran shrugged. "Everyone has their secrets. What they show on the outside isn't necessarily the same as what's really on the inside."

Gran and Travis shared a look, short but meaningful.

Secrets, indeed.

"All I know," Gran continued, "is what was going on in Jake's insides was hardly rainbows and puppies last week when I went to the bank. I already told Detective Palmer all about it."

"What happened?" I asked.

Gran tapped her two spoons together and set them inside her empty bowl. "This happened two days ago. Jake was standing across the street from the bank talking on his cell phone, carrying on and on and using words I dare not repeat at the dinner table."

"What was he saying?" Travis asked, glancing at me. "The PG version, of course."

"I don't like to eavesdrop, but it was kind of hard not to hear him. It was something about a candle. Something wasn't there when the candle burned, he said...or something. But honestly, I don't see how a burning candle could make someone that upset. I'm sure there was more to it, and he might've gotten to the point faster if he hadn't used so much colorful language in between."

"What bank did you go to?" I asked.

Travis clasped his hands on the table and leaned toward me. "That's important why?"

"Jake was standing across the street from her," I explained. "Next to a candle shop maybe? There are several in Belle's Cove."

Gran wagged a finger in the air. "Come to think of it, you could be right. I was coming out of Civic Bank on Main Street. Almost Flame-ous is across the street and down a little. Maybe he was screaming at them on the phone. Or about them."

"Is getting screamed at over a burning candle enough to make someone a murderer?" I asked.

Gran shrugged. "I don't know. I've never murdered anyone, but I suppose all it takes is one second to snap when you've had enough." She picked up her tea and gave me a wide grin. "The candle shop. That was a genius connection. Are you sure you're not also an ace detective?"

"Hardly," I said with a chuckle. It wasn't really a genius connection either. After all, candles had to come from somewhere. But what could Jake have been so upset about? I finished up my peach iced tea and sighed. "That was too good. Thank you, but I suppose I should be going."

Gran reached across the table and folded my hands into hers. "This has been so great, Victoria. Please know you're more than welcome here any time. Travis and I would love to have you."

She sounded so earnest that it broke my heart all over again that she'd lost so much—not only her son, but her son from another mother, my dad.

"I'm really glad I came," I said, glancing at Travis, "though I admit it wasn't easy."

He nodded. "Few things are."

"Wise words."

"I have plenty more words that are pretty wise too," he said and offered me his hand. "Come on. I'll walk you to your car."

"That's not necessary." I stood from the table. "I'm pretty sure I can find it."

"Showing you out is what a Southern gentleman does," he insisted, standing too.

I pushed in my chair, waved to Gran, and started down the hall with Travis tailing me. "That's great. Do you know any gentlemen around here?"

He snorted a laugh. So did Gran behind us, followed by a dramatic, "Mm-*hmm*."

Whatever that meant.

Outside, we stepped off the porch, and a soft, peach-scented breeze teased through my turquoise hair. I'd just eaten and drunk my fill of peaches, yet I didn't think I could ever grow tired of that sweet smell.

"Could I interest you in a walk through the grove before you go?" Travis asked. "There's something magical about peaches under a full moon."

I opened my car door then turned, a solid "No" on the tip of my tongue, but stopped when he casually leaned against my hood. The full moon did something magical with him too. It cast half of him in shadow, the other in silvery light. The way both halves gazed at me was a complete mystery because I didn't hate it. I didn't know what to do about it either.

"Tempting, but no thanks," I told him. "I miss my cat."

He shook his head, a smile stuck to his mouth. "Always so honest about everything."

"I am what I am." I shrugged. "Flaws and all."

"You're not flawed. You're..." He strode toward my open car door, and what had once been lightyears between us shrank to less than a foot. "Different. Refreshing."

My heartbeat stuttered with the compliment. He could charge the air with the way he looked at me all he wanted though. Maybe he wasn't who I thought he was, but I wouldn't let him change my mind about one thing.

"Flattery will get you nowhere." I ducked into my car and slammed the door on all these weird feelings and unwanted responses he triggered. "I'm still not buying Speedy Zone from you."

His chuckle, as warm as the peach-scented air, filtered in through my open window as I drove away.

Chapter Seven

Commandment Eleven: Thou Shall Not Wake the Cat

IF SPEEDY ZONE WERE cursed, then Sunray's was doomed.

It was a gorgeous Monday morning with happy birds tweeting to each other. Boxy whistled while he puttered about in the garage. It might as well have been pouring toxic squids from the sky though. We'd been open since seven, and not one customer had shown up for their appointment. No one had dropped by to complain about squeaky brakes or leaking fluids. Not one single person was brave enough to walk past without spying me first leaning against the frame of the open garage, then flying across the street to the opposite sidewalk. It was as though they thought I'd go full troll if they dare to pass.

Given my mood, I just might.

"We've caught the murder plague," I muttered.

"Nonsense," Boxy said from inside the shop. "We've had slow days before."

"Nothing like this. Not in June when people are traveling more. I wonder if Speedy Zone is slow too. If they are, where is everyone taking their cars? Out of town?" I blew out a slow breath and reminded myself to stay calm and not look like a crazy person in case anyone saw me.

"Well..." Boxy grunted, stooping to pick up a dropped lug nut, and then eyed Studmuffin asleep on the shelves. Pretty sure my familiar had swatted it off the shelves to make room for sleepy time. "Call He Who Only Comes Out at Night and ask him since you're best friends with him now."

I rolled my eyes skyward. "I had cobbler with his gran. That's hardly best-friend status."

Boxy strolled up next to me, juggling the lug nut in his non-cane hand. "Then what is it?"

"It's I-will-tolerate-him status so people don't think I want to murder his employees and business," I explained.

Just then, Mrs. Salmon of the exclusive Salmon Ridge Estates and her diamond-collared dog strolled up the sidewalk, stopped short, and nearly flung themselves into traffic in their rush to get away. I knew her by reputation only, and she had her surgically-shaped nose pressed flat to the town's gossip. I'd bet money she only heard me say, "I want to murder his employees and business."

Wonderful. Simply wonderful. No more words for me today or ever.

Boxy nodded. "So that's what cobbler means, huh? That you'll tolerate him?"

I turned and nodded, my lips sealed shut.

"He is kind of handsome, though, isn't he?" Boxy asked.

"I... He's... *What*? No. I don't know." Yeah, my self-imposed word ban had lasted two seconds, and all for that flustered mess.

Boxy grinned. "Uh-huh."

"Uh-huh what?"

"Just uh-huh," he said, shrugging.

"Fine, but I'll uh-huh you about Ms. Stevenson too. Is she why you're in a skippy mood today?"

"Maybe..."

I gasped. "I *knew* it."

He looked around us and then leaned in conspiratorially. "Promise me you won't freak out if I tell you a secret?"

"Nope. No way, I can't promise that."

After leaning his cane against his hip, he brought up his hands and exploded them into jazz fingers. "I'm meeting her for decaf coffee Friday night."

I screeched, which made Studmuffin jerk awake. Ohhh no. Waking him was a felony punishable by kitty judgement glares and a cuddle ban that could last for hours, but I couldn't help it. This was the first moment of glee for the day. "Coffee where? Coffee like a coffee date?"

"Just coffee, and *she* asked *me*." He beamed. "Can you believe it? She asked this old man to go out and get coffee. With her. With Isabella Stevenson, the best librarian and bookmobile driver in Belle's Cove."

I grinned like a maniac. "I'm happy for you. Truly."

"Thanks." He shrugged like it was no big deal, but of course it was. "We'll see how it goes."

"It will go perfectly," I assured him. An idea struck then, and one look at the empty parking lot and garage confirmed I should do it. His good news had inspired me to try to find a little of my own. "Hey, do you think you can handle things around here for a bit? I need to run an errand."

"Go on," he said and mopped his face with his railroad cap. "This place will be packed by the time you get back. You'll see."

"I don't believe you, but thanks for humoring me." I risked a look at Studmuffin. His turbo death glare aimed right for my head. I didn't even have to ask if he was coming with me or not. Poor fluffer-stinker. I'd have to bribe him with treats for days.

I could've walked the few short blocks to Almost Flame-ous, but I hadn't heard the purr of an engine up close and personal all morning long. I was worried I might go into withdrawal, so I took Bernadette.

I had never been inside Almost Flame-ous, but as soon as I pulled up in front of the little shop, I realized that had been a mistake. Candles of all shapes and sizes and colors burned in the storefront window on a beautiful tabletop display with more lit candles hanging in an iron chandelier above. Next to the window, two tall wooden pillars that had been carved in swirling, candle-like twists flanked the entrance. A collection of red and orange ribbons were attached to the wicks on top to create the effect of burning. The breeze caught them just right and fluttered and flickered them like real fire. Inside, I expected to be suffocated by all the different scents, but only a light, flowery smell wafted through the store.

The tall, skinny woman behind the counter who looked about my age smiled. "Can I help you?"

"Yeah, do you know Jake Williams?" I asked, cutting right to the chase, or the wick in this case.

The woman frowned. "The name sounds familiar, but I'm not sure. Why?"

"One second and I'll show you a picture of him," I said, fumbling for my cell in my purse. After a quick search on the internet, I shoved a picture of him under her nose. "I just wondered if he'd ever been here before."

"I don't remember seeing him, no." She peered closer at the picture. "It says here he was *murdered*?"

"On Friday," I said with a long sigh. "Do you work here all the time or...?"

"I don't," she said. "I have one part-time employee who works evenings and weekends. I could ask her if she's seen him if you want."

"That'd be great, thanks." I told her to contact Sunray's with any information, bought two pillar candles that were much too pretty to ever burn, and left the store.

Outside, I squinted into the sun toward the direction of Civic Bank. It was almost half a block away, but I suppose if Jake had been yelling into his cell, Gran could've heard some of what he said. Maybe he wasn't upset about candles, but something that sounded like candles? Mantels, maybe? Burning vandals? Yearning for sandals? Or maybe this was the wrong candle shop altogether.

What was I even doing anyway? It wasn't my job to track down clues about Jake's murder, and yet there

I stood on the sidewalk, Googling the addresses of the other four candle shops in town.

Wait a minute, though. I had candles at home that I had no idea where they came from. It was like one day they'd just appeared, and I'd been too distracted by one thing or another to pay much attention. They'd probably been a gift. Or they'd come through the same void that ate socks in the dryer. Candles in exchange for socks. Not a bad deal.

Okay, I really needed to stop eating so much sugar. It was rotting my brain.

Maybe if I got a good look at the candle, I'd be able to tell why he'd been screaming about it two days before his murder. Maybe I could also tell whether it had leaped through the dryer void or not. At the very least, it could have a shop name on the bottom sticker like the two I'd just bought.

After another Google search, I brought up his address, which was only a couple blocks away. It wasn't as though I had much else to do.

As I opened the door to Bernadette, my phone rumbled in my purse with the sound of a revving engine. That meant it was Boxy. When I swiped to answer it, Studmuffin's continued death glare drilled through the screen in a video call.

I sagged against my car laughing. This wasn't the first time he'd borrowed Boxy's phone to call me. "I will never wake you from another nap again, I promise. Please don't be mad."

Boxy's railroad cap bobbed behind Studmuffin's head. "Did you get to my phone again? I just changed the password on that thing."

I erupted into laughter again, drawing looks and then double-takes from people strolling past. Then of course they booked it away from the laughing, murderous troll lady.

Boxy's face appeared behind Studmuffin's. "Checking up on you, is he?"

"More like reminding me who's boss," I said, trying to contain myself. "I just have one more stop to make. Is it busy there yet?"

He scratched his neck as he looked around. "Busy in terms of inventory?"

"No."

"Not yet, but they're coming." He made a fist and pounded it against his chest. "You gotta keep that hope alive, Vic."

I sighed, but it was hard to feel down while talking to two of my favorite creatures. Even though one of them hadn't blinked this entire call because he was so busy piercing me with yellow-green-eyed daggers. "Yeah, I'll try. I'll be there—"

Studmuffin's paw swiped the phone, and the call ended. My familiar just hung up on me.

My stomach ached with laughter as I folded myself into my car. I'd have to really bribe him with treats and cuddles and beg his forgiveness. Boxy, being a quiet ninja, had never awakened Studmuffin and suffered his wrath. Lucky guy.

Feeling much lighter than I had all morning, I drove the short trip to Jake's house. He lived in a simple rectangular house next to other rectangular houses. There was nothing different about his other than a swirling pinwheel jutting up from the top of his mailbox at the curb and seashell wind chimes hanging next to the front door. The grass had been trimmed not long ago because clippings breezed over the driveway, and I sneezed my way to the front door. I hoped a fresh-cut lawn meant someone was here. I didn't even know if he was married or if the crazy girlfriend Travis had mentioned lived with Jake.

I rang the doorbell and waited. Seconds later, a woman about my age with frizzy, shoulder-length blonde hair and red-rimmed eyes opened the door.

"Hi," I said as gently as I could. "I'm Victoria Fox. I knew Jake in school. He was a good guy."

The woman gave me a hard look. "Okay..."

"I just wondered if I could come in and talk to you about him."

Her mouth twisted like she'd just tasted something sour. "Now's not a great time. I'm leaving to work a double shift at The Belly Up Diner."

"Just a few quick questions, then. Did Jake have any candles?"

She blinked at me. "Candles? What is this about?"

"I don't know exactly. A friend of mine overheard Jake on his phone upset about burned candles. Was he big into candles?"

The woman rubbed her hands together nervously or as though she wasn't quite sure what else to do with them. "Why is that a question for you to ask about my fiancé? Are you with the police?"

Fiancé? Yet there was no engagement ring on her finger.

"I'm not with the police. I just—" What could I say? I sure couldn't tell her I was a suspect and that most of the town thought I murdered Jake. "Like I said, I'm a friend. I just want to know what happened."

"Then let the police figure it out," she snapped and then slammed the door in my face.

Yep, I deserved that. I hadn't really had a plan other than demanding to know how great Jake's candle game was. I wouldn't have let me in either.

I should've had a better excuse, a reason to be poking my nose around, rather than showing up like a creeper and asking strange questions.

I wasn't very good at this, uh, whatever this was I was doing. Not proving my innocence, that was for sure.

While I dragged myself back to Bernadette at the curb and tried to fight off another sneeze attack, the garage door opened behind me. It was her, Jake's fiancée, leaving for a double shift at The Belly Up Diner. Leaving the house all by its lonesome. It would be a real shame if I didn't take advantage of this opportunity, snap a few photos inside windows, and hope that one of them was of an easily recognizable candle. Of course it would be a greater shame if I got caught.

I ducked into Bernadette as the woman backed her light-gray Honda Accord out. Hmm, light gray could be mistaken for white. Then I stared hard at what she was wearing—a bright yellow jacket.

Chapter Eight
Cat Burglars Need Friends Too

"YOU WANT TO *WHAT*?" Travis jabbed each word into his phone like an accusatory finger. "Speak slower so I have a second to find my jaw. It fell off somewhere between yellow jacket and you thinking about trespassing."

I gulped down a breath of air and then funneled it out, long and steady. I sat inside Bernadette next to the air pump at a nearby gas station while trying to work out what to do next. It was broad daylight, hardly the time to do any snooping at Jake's house. In the back of my mind, though, I was making plans to do just that.

"Jake's fiancée didn't seem to know anything about burning candles, but what if it's all an act?" I lowered my voice even though my car windows were only open a crack. "What if she killed him?"

"Then that's yet another reason why you shouldn't go there tonight to take pictures," Travis said.

I could practically hear him rolling his eyes.

"But she won't be there. Double shift at The Belly Up Diner, remember? I just want to look into a few windows and see if I can find something, anything, a kernel of evidence to hand over and save Sunray's." My voice cracked a little, and I prayed he wouldn't notice over the phone. Too much emotion was what happened when I poured out my heart, and my shop *was* my heart.

"Why are you telling me all of this?" Travis asked gently. "Why did you call *me*? Do you want me to talk you out of it?"

"You can't talk me out of it. I just want you to know my reasoning so if this blows up in my face, you'll know I had good intentions. You're one of the very few who believes I'm innocent."

"And Boxy? Have you told him?"

"I will. I tell him everything. But even though he's a ninja and would do really well sneaking around at night, I won't agree to it. This already looks bad for me and Sunray's, but if he's mixed up in all this, too, it will look doubly bad."

A long pause followed, so long I checked my phone to make sure the battery hadn't died. "Did you... Did you..." Disbelief tinged his voice. "Did you just say he's a *ninja*?"

I sighed. Honest to a fault, I was. Think like Yoda now, I do. Ugh, stay focused. "We're all something, Travis. I'm a witch. Boxy's a ninja. You're a—"

"Farmer who happens to own Speedy Zone," he said in a rush. "Nothing else."

"Right..." People who had nothing to hide *never* acted like they had something to hide, for obvious reasons. Not like Travis. Not like Gran either. What was it? And why did they think I wouldn't understand after I'd shared so much with them already?

Like my dad used to say though—let's pick one seat-belt-free rollercoaster at a time.

"If we were to go to Jake's," he continued, "big *if*, what time would that be?"

"After dark but before ten, so..." My eyes widened. "Wait. Did you just say we? You're coming?"

Travis let out a bone-weary sigh. "You honestly think I'm going to let you go to Jake's house, where a possible murderer might live, by yourself?"

"Um...yes?"

A banging sounded over the line, like maybe his head on his desk. "What time should I pick you up?"

"You shouldn't." I shook my head hard even though he couldn't see me. "This isn't a date. I'll meet you at Gas, Guzzles, & Go at dusk. It's only a couple blocks away from Jake's house."

"Okay, but I didn't imply it was a date. It's you and me committing a crime."

"In some parts of the world, that's called a date," I said. "Besides, I doubt you've gotten your car exorcised yet, have you?"

"It's running a little rough is all."

"You can come by Sunray's any time, and I'll fix it for you." Whoa. Even I was stunned at my offer, but he'd just agreed to trespass with me. It was sort of a fair trade.

"Careful," he said, and I could hear the smile in his voice. "I believe that could also be called a date. See you at seven, Victoria."

"I said dusk, not seven. Eight thirty or so."

"Hm, I thought I did say dusk. But now that you mention it, would you like to meet at seven for gas station sushi and two extra-large bags of Cheetos while we take the long way to Jake's? There's a wildlife refuge nearby with a duck pond that's spectacular at sunset. It'll be my treat."

"Gas station sushi and Cheetos sound like a disaster waiting to happen." I laughed and shook my head. "*Dusk*, Travis. And don't wear any bright colors."

AFTER A LONG DAY of no customers, I planned to leave for Gas, Guzzles, & Go a little before dusk. My stomach swam with nervous little worms, so there would be no Cheetos or sushi for me, thanks.

Boxy had already gone home, but he'd kept fixing me with his one good eye and the fake one, both of which could see right through me. He knew something was up. Usually I would try to explain since I told him everything, but we were co-conspirators at Sunray's, not crimes. If I had to, I would bend over backwards to keep him out of this.

Studmuffin trotted up to me as I opened the door to Bernadette.

I groaned and deflated a little. "Oh no, this is definitely not the trip for you. Why don't you stay home and enjoy the whole place to yourself? You know where the catnip is. Go nuts."

Ignoring me completely, he leaped into Bernadette, stepped over to the passenger seat, and tapped his paw on the driver seat as if to tell me he wasn't getting any younger.

"This could be dangerous," I hissed. "I don't like the idea of you and danger mixed together."

He tilted his head at me and gave me a hard stare as if my brain's engine had stalled. Maybe it had. And maybe I could use some magical help from my familiar tonight to keep us from getting caught.

"I get no say in this, do I?" I asked, scooting in next to him. "You're lucky I love you."

He head-butted my arm as he climbed into my lap, and after clasping my seat belt around the both of us, we were finally off.

Of course, by the time we pulled in, Travis was already there at the far edge of the lot. He leaned against his car with the setting sun at his back. It lit his sandy-blond hair to a golden red and flecked the windows of his bright yellow Mustang with perfect rainbows. How could someone always look like they were posing in a model photo shoot when they really weren't?

As soon as Studmuffin saw him, he pressed his paw to the glass. Smiling, Travis waved back.

"You two," I muttered. "I'll have to get you both matching BFF necklaces, won't I?"

Studmuffin chirped in agreement and then burst out of the car as soon as I opened the door.

"Hey, bud," Travis said to him. "Good to see you again."

My familiar mewed and trilled and told him about his day, all the while keeping his distance from Travis's boots. Even he knew this was hardly the time to get sleepy.

"He insisted on coming. I insisted he stay home," I said as I clambered out of Bernadette. "Guess who won that argument."

Travis waved my worries away. "The more the merrier. Have you eaten?"

"The answer to that is always yes."

"Still hungry?"

"Yet another always yes. Why?"

He reached into his open window, withdrew a small bag of Cheetos, and tossed it underhanded at me. I snatched it out of the air with one hand.

"Ready, Willie Mays?" he asked, his smile growing wider.

"I don't know who that is, but yes, let's get going." I pointed at our cars. "You think this is too obvious, your car and mine parked next to each other?"

He shrugged and started slowly up the sidewalk in the direction of Jake's house. "As long as our cars don't try anything with each other, I think they'll be fine. We're far enough away from his house that I don't think anyone will notice."

Studmuffin and I fell into step next to him. "How are you so calm about everything?" I asked Travis.

"Well, I just ate gas station sushi and a bag of Cheetos. It has a way of threatening my nerves with a bunch of 'or elses.'" He gave me a long, sweeping look from head to toe. "Plus, you look nice."

"I look like an over-sugared, over-caffeinated squirrel," I said, ripping open the Cheetos. "But thanks."

I was dressed in all black to blend in with the coming night and wore my long turquoise hair swept up underneath a Belle's Cove High School softball cap. Nothing special, but still, I appreciated the compliment.

"Studmuffin, stay on the inner part of the sidewalk," I warned, "or I will threaten *you* with a bunch of 'or elses.'"

Surprisingly, as we continued our evening stroll, he stuck to my right leg while Travis kept brushing my left shoulder, the side closest to the road. It was a narrow sidewalk and Studmuffin despised setting one paw on prickly grass, so I felt a little sandwiched. Good thing I had Cheetos to go with that sandwich. I munched on one as we walked in silence for a bit.

"How was business today?" I asked as casually as I could, which wasn't casual at all.

"A little slow but good. Some people came to show their respects to Jake as well as get their car worked on. His death has really taken a toll on this town." Travis glanced at me. "How was business for you?"

"What business?" I frowned at how bitter I sounded, but I didn't care. "I had all morning to go to Jake's house and all afternoon to think about going back to Jake's house tonight." I'd also answered the one phone call we received from Almost Flame-ous. The part-time employee hadn't seen Jake there either.

"I'm sorry," he said with a long sigh. It sounded like he really meant it. "The funeral is Wednesday if you'd like to come."

"Yeah, I might."

We slowed as we neared an intersection, and I kept one eye on Studmuffin and the other on any oncoming traffic. A feat, let me tell you. We didn't go for walks like this, so naturally, I didn't have a leash. Even if I did, I had absolutely no say in how my cat lived his life. Hopefully we weren't breaking any leash laws. Hopefully, as not only a cat but a witch's familiar, he knew that roads equaled bad.

Once we crossed with all parts still intact, I said, "I'm curious to see everyone who knew Jake in the same place. One of them has to know something."

Travis nodded. "It sounds like there will be hundreds of people there. Finding a clue might be like finding a needle in a haystack."

"Needles are sharp. I'll find it." I looked around to see if there was anyone outside their houses who might overhear, but we seemed alone. "Besides, I'm hoping tonight will help us. Me. Help *me*."

Travis grinned. "I'm here, aren't I?"

"You are." I crunched on another Cheeto. "Thank you."

Studmuffin paused briefly at a dandelion growing at the edge of someone's yard. Then he licked it as if to say hello.

Travis and I both laughed as the cat sauntered toward us with a rare big grin on his face.

"We don't get out much," I admitted.

"Me neither."

"Yeah, I never used to see you in the daylight, if ever. Not that I was looking for you or anything. Boxy and I even had a nickn—" I broke off when I saw Travis's expression.

Not only was he frowning so hard that his forehead wrinkled, but also his shoulders were bunched to his ears as if to physically ward off everything I was saying.

"Are you all right?" I said in a rush.

Travis opened his mouth to say something, but then I noticed that Studmuffin had stopped flicking my leg with his tale as we walked. He stood behind me a little ways. His fur had bushed out along his spine while he stood stone-still. He sniffed the air once, twice. Then, he tore off down the sidewalk as though the demon who lived in Travis's Mustang had given chase.

"Studmuffin, no!" I shouted.

My muscles fused together for one shocked second, then Travis and I were sprinting after him. Even with his white murder mittens and white patterns on his back, he blended into the dark so well it was hard to see him. He zipped right around the corner ahead.

"He's heading toward Jake's house," I said between huffs and puffs.

"He must know something we don't." Travis hardly sounded winded as we ran.

"He should also know that I'll ground him for the rest of his nine"—I grunted in pain—"lives."

This whole running thing? Not a fan. Of course I'd do it for my ornery Studmuffin though.

He tiptoed into the yard at the side of Jake's house, trying with all his might not to touch the prickly grass under his paws. Now that he was going slower, I poured on more speed to catch him. By the time we got to the neighbor's, though, my familiar had already disappeared.

"Studmuffin," I hissed. My shoulders drooped. Why was he doing this?

Just then, the front door of Jake's house popped open silently.

"Down!" Travis hauled me behind the neighbor's red Subaru. We peered over the trunk.

A furry, naughty little head poked out from inside Jake's house.

"Bad, *bad* kitty," I whispered.

"*Smart* kitty," Travis said, his voice filled with awe. "How did he do that?"

I shot Travis a warning look, but he didn't even notice.

It might have been a trick of the moonlight, but it sure looked like Studmuffin put a paw to his mouth as if to tell us, "Shh." Then he disappeared into the dark house.

"That cat is seriously damaging my Cheeto calm," I said through gritted teeth.

Travis stood in a half-crouch. "We have to go get him. You wanted a look inside anyway. If we get caught, you can blame it on your burglar cat."

"*If* we get caught?" I waved my hands in Boxy's jazzy style. "Look at my fingers. I'm a walking orange fingerprint."

"Ah, I can fix that." With a flourish, Travis withdrew a small plastic bottle from his jacket pocket. "It's hand sanitizer. Gran won't let me anywhere near the house without it after I've been working on the farm."

He squeezed a large dollop into my hands, and I rubbed it in. Eventually, it flaked the Cheetos dust to the ground.

"Thanks. It's like you came prepared, or like you've done this kind of thing before," I told him. "Are we really doing this?"

"Well..." He pocketed the hand sanitizer again. "When one door closes, another opens. That seems pretty relevant right now."

He was right. We may not get this opportunity again. Even if we did at some point, it might be too late to save Sunray's.

I took in a deep, shaky breath and released it. "Okay, let's go."

We rose from out of the shadows and crept inside a dead man's—and possibly his killer's—house.

Chapter Nine

An Unacceptable Number of Severed Heads

WITH ONE FLICK OF Studmuffin's tail, Jake's front door closed behind us.

Travis immediately dropped to his hands and knees and powered on the flashlight app on his phone.

"What are you doing?" I asked, barely a whisper.

He pointed right through the living room toward the back kitchen wall. "We don't want to be visible through that window."

"Through that very *open* window." I shot a glare at Studmuffin, but he'd conveniently disappeared again.

Sighing, I dropped next to Travis, using his light to scan the house.

"They really like furniture here," he muttered.

No joke. Bookcases, end tables, a desk, a TV stand, couches, and chairs crowded end to end around the perimeter of the living room, minus the three hallways and the front door. The effect made the room much smaller than I expected.

"They really like candles too." They were everywhere, in jars, inside metal fixtures, floating in shallow bowls filled with water and shiny silver rocks. Pretty, but nothing like the magical candle store, Almost Flame-ous.

I picked a candle up using the bottom of my shirt and flipped it over. Safe-Mart the sticker on the bottom read. Another one read the same thing.

"Any old burning candle wouldn't make him scream into his phone, though," I whispered. "It has to be a special candle."

Something wasn't there when the candle burned, Gran Black had overheard him say. Light? A wick? *What?*

"Take a look at this." Travis had crawled over to a desk and was shining his phone on top. The light bounced back and hit the crease between his eyebrows. "It's a calendar. On the day Jake died, he wrote two things and their times. Both things were during his lunchbreak."

As I moved toward him, I caught sight of Studmuffin's tail flinging dust down on us from on top of a tall bookshelf. I rolled my eyes. Pretty sure the highlight of tonight for him would be watching us crawl around on the floor like pesky ants.

"You're sure it's Jake's handwriting?" I asked Travis, coming up behind him.

"He helps—helped—me do inventory because other than Celeste, the front counter lady, he was the only one with legible handwriting." He shrugged.

"Call me old-fashioned, but I still do things with paper and pen."

"I get it," I whispered. "I still listen to CDs."

"Yeah?"

Nodding, I stood on my knees to snap a photo of the date in question, Friday, June 17.

12:10 – Henderson's

12:30 – Boro Yate

"Henderson's is a barbershop, isn't it?" I asked.

"It is." Travis tapped his chin. "Boro Yate. I know that from somewhere."

"That lawyer here in town with the commercial." I cleared my throat for my whispered, sing-song demo. "Call zero-zero-zero, five-five-five-fiverrr. Boro Yate than neverrrr."

Travis blinked at me. "That's terrible."

"Hey, I didn't write it. Some annoyingly clever person did to get it stuck in my head." Wait, was he talking about my singing voice or the commercial? I tapped my phone where the picture of Jake's calendar still displayed. "So why was he going to see a lawyer?"

"I don't know," Travis said. "It could be about anything."

I dropped down to all fours again and looked around. "Let's find more about his fiancée."

We searched while trying not to touch anything and then ventured into the kitchen. Two empty bowls sat on the floor in front of the oven, both stamped with a bone. Bones meant dogs, but I was sure if they were here, they would've announced their presence by now.

Travis headed straight for the cabinets and drawers. I headed toward the refrigerator. The inside of someone's refrigerator could tell a lot about someone. How did I know this? I only had a few cans of diet soda in mine. Studmuffin stored all of his baking ingredients inside some magical ether, I supposed. Still, opening Jake's refrigerator would bring in a lot of light.

It was worth it, just a glimpse. I blocked the door as much as I could with my body and used my shirt to open it. Glass jars rattled slightly in the door, and three opened ketchup bottles sat right up front on the top shelf. The rest of it looked normal. No severed heads or anything.

What a disappointment. I mean in terms of finding a murderer, not that I wanted to open a refrigerator someday and see someone's head. Well, maybe just once.

"Unacceptable." I quickly shut it and dropped back to the floor. "Find anything?"

"About a dozen bottle openers and a toaster that's seen better days," Travis whispered. "Not exactly the things murders—or murderers—are made of."

"Let's check the rest of the house."

We crawled back through the living room where Studmuffin was carefully grooming his murder mittens on the bookshelf. By the light of Travis's phone shining in front of us, I could only see my familiar's shadow and his glowing yellow-green eyes shimmering with glee.

"Yeah, yeah," I whispered, crawling past him. "Laugh it up now, Studmuffin, because it's all fun and games until your favorite witch gets arrested."

Travis glanced over his shoulder at me. "Are you still considered a witch, though, if you don't use magic?"

"Watch it." I slapped his backside since it was right in front of me as we crawled down another hallway that led to the back of the house. "Now's hardly the time."

"Just wondering. And yes, your familiar is having entirely too much fun. He acts like he's done this before."

I shrugged. "I'm just his chauffeur. That's all I know."

We stopped in the hall outside a bathroom. Travis shined his light over blue tile, a blue bathtub, even a blue toilet.

I checked the cupboards under the sink but found only cleaning supplies and an empty bucket. "There has to be another bathroom here."

"Why does there have to be?" Travis asked.

"Where are all Jake's fiancée's things? Other than the candles, there's no feminine touches to the house and no feminine things. Women have *things*, Travis."

"Yes, I'm aware of said things," he said wryly. "If his fiancée did murder him, why do it at Speedy Zone? Why not here?"

"Because it would be a little more obvious who did it here. And if you rule out the weird yellow jacket choice to wear to a murder, I'm beginning to think it wasn't a crime of passion. This was deliberate. Someone knew exactly what they were doing when they removed the relief valve on the hydraulics system while Jake was working on the truck that killed him."

Travis nodded. "If she was there, if she was wearing her yellow jacket, and everyone knows Jake's death was a murder, why wear the jacket around town, then?"

"Good point. She's not acting like a guilty person, is she?"

"No. Let's keep looking."

The bedroom at the end of this hall turned out to be uninteresting except for the little jump scare we gave ourselves with the mirror in the corner of the room. I didn't know what terror was until I saw ourselves crawl toward our other selves. Good times. Once we recovered, we found as much excitement as we could handle with the empty unmade bed against the wall, some weights on the floor, and even more candles on a dresser.

As we crawled through the living room toward the third and final hallway, a rustle outside the front door stopped us cold.

Travis looked at me with wide eyes. "Some-one's—"

"Coming," I hissed.

Hot-cold dread flooded down into my stomach. We scrambled down the hallway. My heart leapfrogged into my throat as a key jiggled in the lock. If we were caught here, that was it. The end of Sunray's. I prayed to the car gods that would *not* happen.

We dodged into the room just as the door opened. Where to now? If that was Jake's fiancée, would she murder us too? And what about Studmuffin? Where was he? Panic fused to my lungs and made it hard to breathe.

Travis powered off his phone, but I could see well enough. As quietly as I could, I opened the closet door across the room with the hem of my T-shirt then slipped inside. Travis followed, his bulky shoulders knocking into empty hangers. Wincing, I shut the door quickly.

We went still. Moonlight from the window to the right angled into the wooden slats on the closet door. Beyond this bedroom, I couldn't see anything. Why wasn't whoever entered the house turning on any lights?

A bump-crash came from the living room then the sound of a struck match. Soon, light flickered from one of the many candles out there.

Travis was wedged so he faced me, one hand looped through the empty hangers to keep them from clicking together and the other keeping the door shut. His breaths came out in quiet bursts and tickled the side of my nose.

My nose tickling worsened, and not because Travis was breathing all over me. Something smelled funny in here. I was more concerned with how painfully my right shoulder dug into the closet wall though. Something lumpy under my feet upset my balance. I glanced down and found shoes, or the shapes of shoes rather. I righted my feet on solid ground and stirred the air with more of that smell.

That was grass I smelled, the freshly cut kind that always made me sneeze. Oh *no*. Now was not the time for this nonsense.

The lit candle from the living room floated toward us. No, not floated. Carried. A stocky man I'd never seen before with a dark red vest and a deep frown roamed his gaze over the room.

My eyes watered. I clamped my mouth shut and slapped my hand over it for reinforcement. This was it. Death by sneeze, or because of one. I was sure of it.

The man eyed the closet for a moment but then barged toward the dresser below the window, which was covered with an assortment of candles. He flipped them over, scraped the dried, melted wax with his fingernails, even crashed one against the side of the dresser to split it apart.

He was looking for something *inside* the candle. That's what was missing? Some sort of object hidden within a candle? But what? Whatever it was, he didn't seem to be finding it. He dumped the broken candle pieces into a drawer and then stormed out of the room.

The tickling in my nose lessened. Slowly, I let myself relax as much as I could inside a closet I had no business being trapped in. Crisis averted.

Just kidding. The sneeze came back with a vengeance as they sometimes do.

Travis slapped his hand over mine over my mouth to help me catch it. It sounded like a tiny mouse squeak, the equivalent of a lion's roar in the quiet house.

In the hallway, the man spun around and stared.

Travis and I stilled. My heartbeat sped to a steady hum between my ears.

The flickering candle the man carried threw moving shadows all over him. He took a step toward us.

Ohhhh no. I threw my hand over Travis's, which was still over my other one *and* my mouth. Now would be a really great time to use magic without exploding anything. The only spell I'd ever done successfully was levitating myself though. I didn't see how that could help me now.

"Is someone there?" the man asked in a gravelly voice. Another step closer.

If only I could teleport us out of here or fling some sort of spell at him. Or maybe distract him with a glitter thunderstorm.

A terrible yowl sounded from behind him, one I was super familiar with. It was the same yowl

Studmuffin used at three a.m. when he had the urge to sing me the song of his species while running at top speed. I called it the vrooms because cars, but they're also known as the zooms.

He yowled again. A small bushy shadow zipped round and round the living room furniture like the floor was lava.

"What in the world? Get out of here!" The man darted toward him, but Studmuffin streaked down the hallway toward the first bedroom we'd explored. The man shot after him.

Saved by the cat. Time to skedaddle.

Travis and I removed all hands from my mouth, joined two of them, and got out of there fast. At the end of the short hall, we paused and glanced down the other. In the room at the end, Studmuffin leaped all over the bed. The man shouted at him and made attempts to grab him. Then, as though he wasn't the least bit concerned—probably because he wasn't—my familiar winked at me.

He'd be fine, I told myself. He'd be just fine.

Still, a lump formed in my throat as we dashed out of the house on tiptoes. We didn't stop running until we came to the end of the block. Then we hid behind a large black truck on the side of the road.

"Let's never do that again." I bent double with my hands on my knees and sucked air, completely done with tonight. "I think my heart imploded. Is that a thing? Because it happened twice in there."

Travis shrugged, hardly winded, and grinned. "I thought it was pretty great, actually. I can't remember the last time I've run for my life like that. It's exhilarating. It reminds you of the importance of living, which is something I've missed..."

"Nope to everything you just said." I peered around the truck for any sign of Studmuffin. "Here lies Victoria Fox. She wanted to be buried in a pyramid, but right here's cool."

Chuckling, Travis caught my gaze and held it. "No, no, you deserve a pyramid."

"Thanks." Just then, I realized that our hands were still tightly clasped. His skin felt warm and safe, too pleasant to pull away from just yet. Plus, I didn't have time, because a loud pop sounded right behind me.

I whirled and then gasped. In the tree behind us stood Studmuffin in his power pose. He lifted one mitten so that I may kiss it.

All my frustrations with him from earlier vanished at the sight of him. I almost wept when I scooped him into a hug and smothered him in kisses. "Are you all right? Never again. You hear me? No more being a bad kitty. Ever."

He swiped his cheek against mine, his loud purr a comfort after the night we'd had, yet that wasn't him agreeing to my "never again." That was a distraction, and he knew it. It was totally working though. I fell for it every time.

I set him down since too much love gave him the vrooms, and we set off into the night like three innocents. Studmuffin's tail curled around my calf, and Travis's fingers still curled around my own.

And you know what? It wasn't awful.

Chapter Ten

Piñatas and Pyramids

THE ONLY GOOD THING about funerals was that deciding what to wear was relatively easy. I owned one simple black dress—short-sleeves, a tie waist, and buttons down the front. A lot less greasy than my usual garb. No heels, just flats. The last thing I needed was to plant my face into a grave in front of everyone. To top it off, I wore a floppy black hat to help hide most of my face. Boxy and I closed Sunray's down Wednesday afternoon, which wasn't saying much since we'd felt closed all week.

My stomach was swamped with nerves since the reason we felt closed would be at Jake's funeral. How, after all these years of fixing cars honestly and quickly the *first* time, could all of Belle's Cove turn their backs on me? I hadn't even been charged with murder, just questioned once at the scene of the crime. Still, they didn't trust me. It stung, and I was about to go face all of them.

Boxy grinned as I stepped down the final stair into Sunray's waiting area. He looked quite dapper in his black suit, tie, bowler hat, and the fancy dragon cane he reserved for special occasions. Studmuffin was sitting across the little table from him with his murder mittens crossed politely on top.

Boxy stood and stuck out his hand. "The name's Boxy. Nice to meet you. Are you new to town?"

I snorted. "Hardy-har-har. You didn't recognize me without the grease stains?"

"That, and it's rare to see you in a dress. You clean up well." He wrapped me up into a warm, one-armed side hug. "You don't have to be nervous. We're a united front, remember?"

"Always." I hugged him back, so grateful he was on my team. "Did I interrupt you and Studmuffin reminiscing about the good old days?"

"We were just catching up." Boxy rocked back on his heels and lifted his eyebrows. "He had a lot to tell me."

Alarms blared inside my head. "Oh, did he?"

Studmuffin slow-blinked at me as innocently as he could, which wasn't innocent at all. He and Boxy had a special familiar/ninja relationship I don't think I was meant to understand. Both of them would often clam up and stiffen when I walked into the room like I'd interrupted them. While I'd never heard Studmuffin speak, Boxy often talked to him like he would during an actual conversation. He would gasp and laugh and say things like, "Really? I didn't know that."

Surely Studmuffin wouldn't spill about what we did last night. Would he? Of course not. He was just a cat. A cat who baked calorie-free desserts, but still.

"Okay, I'll bite. What did he say?" I asked, faking calm and casual.

Studmuffin fixed me with his no-nonsense stare while stretching his back. He might as well have had a feather sticking out from between his fangs though.

Boxy flipped his wrist up to check his watch with a too-dramatic flourish. "Will you look at the time? We better get going."

"All right, fine. Don't tell me." I pointed at my eyes with two fingers and then at them. "But I'll be watching you both."

The graveside funeral was being held at Maple Grove Cemetery, which made me feel a little bit better about facing the rest of the town. Enclosed spaces invited staring since there wasn't much else to do; outside, people could spread out and focus more on keeping the sun out of their eyes instead of on innocent suspects. At least that's what I told myself as I parked Bernadette outside the cemetery gate. It made sense if I didn't think about it too much.

While white-knuckling the steering wheel, I released a slow breath. "Chin up, make eye contact, and speak from the gut."

Boxy stared at me. "You prepping for a speech or something?"

"Very close. My speech teacher in high school used to remind us of that before presentations. And to also picture everyone naked."

Boxy shuddered. "Terrible advice. That puts the pressure on you. She should've told you to bring a piñata."

I burst out laughing despite our somber location. "What? Why?"

"Everyone would be so distracted by the piñata and what you might do with it at any second. They wouldn't pay you any attention, even if your presentations were the greatest." He jabbed a finger in the air. "Which I'm sure they were."

"Oh. That's kind of brilliant."

"Obviously."

"Bringing a piñata to a funeral doesn't seem right though."

"No, it doesn't, but everyone is distracted enough."

"You're right." I winced and shook my head. "Leave it to me to make Jake's funeral all about me and *my* feelings."

"Nonsense. You're allowed to have feelings, same as everyone else here." He nodded toward the gathering crowd of people walking slowly to the gravesite.

"Thanks, Boxy."

"Don't mention it." He opened his door slowly, keeping his gaze on me. "Ready?"

Not really. "Yeah." With a sigh, I shoved out of my car and then waited for Boxy to join me at the front of the hood.

Dozens of people streamed through the cemetery gates with their heads bowed, some murmuring, others quietly reflective. Some of them I recognized. It would be interesting to see everyone who knew Jake gathered in one place, how they interacted with each other, how they reacted to Jake's funeral. I'd seen in a horror movie that nine times out of ten, victims knew their murderers. No idea if that was accurate or not, but could Jake's murderer be here? Since it seemed like half of Belle's Cove was, then maybe.

Boxy hobbled closer with his cane and offered me his arm. "Looking for someone in particular?"

As I took his arm, I opened my mouth then snapped it shut again. I'd almost blurted I was looking for a murderer, but Boxy didn't need to know that. "Not looking, just thinking. I want to be buried in a pyramid. I'd like everyone to bring a piñata to my funeral. My funeral should be a party. Something unexpected."

"Like you." He nodded. "Well, I won't be there for that, but I do like the idea."

I bumped his shoulder with mine. "Don't say that. Ninjas don't die."

He smiled. "If you say so. Piñatas and a pyramid it is."

We fell quiet as we neared the other mourners, sticking to the back of the crowd. A raised platform sat near the gravesite, covered by a black canopy. Jake's family stood underneath—his parents and two younger sisters. Off to the side, separate from the others, stood Jake's fiancée. I recognized the frizzy blonde hair unraveling from her bun and the nervous way she rubbed her hands together.

The service was short and sweet, punctuated with sniffles and tears. My heart ached for everyone who was hurting. No matter what the killer's motive was, Jake didn't deserve to be murdered. He was a genuinely good guy.

Afterward, Boxy said he wanted to "check on a few people," but really, he was looking for his girlfriend, Ms. Stevenson. I hung back, watching, feeling a little like a creeper, but I had a good reason. Everyone looked and acted appropriately miserable.

There was one woman smiling though. The woman with the perfectly winged eyeliner who worked behind the Speedy Zone counter. She was smiling down at her phone. It didn't mean anything, and it wasn't really out of place. She could have seen an old photo of Jake and was reminiscing. Still, no one else was smiling.

"He's here," a familiar voice whispered.

Travis had come up behind me and grazed my elbow with his fingers.

A strange shiver zipped over my skin, and I pulled away to look up at him. He wore a black suit and tie and of course his ring that looked like it was glowing slightly in the sun. He looked good in a suit, like I might need a spatula to peel my eyes off of him.

Then I remembered what he'd just said. "He who?"

"Red vest." He gave me a meaningful look.

"As in last night's red vest?"

He nodded. "The two nice old ladies standing next to me during the service told me his name is Kole. It turns out he's Jake's uncle. Now"—he pointed both index fingers at me—"you may or may not be surprised that outside the cemetery gates, there's a locksmith truck with Kole's Krafty Keys painted on the outside."

I sucked in a breath. "He's a locksmith."

"You catch on quick."

"If he would've had a key that was given to him to check on the house or whatever, he would've turned on the lights and acted like he should've been there, not sneaking around and hiding candles he'd smashed." I rose on my tiptoes to search for his bald head, but there were too many of those glinting in the sunlight. "Do you think he did it?"

Travis looked around too. "I don't know, but he definitely knows something."

I suddenly had the urge to get a copy of a key made or lock myself out of Sunray's.

"Hey, what can you tell me about the woman who works behind the counter at Speedy Zone?" I asked.

"Who, Celeste?" He shrugged. "She's always on time. She volunteers at the retirement center on weekends where her grandmother lives. Why?"

Before I could answer, Gran Black appeared through the crowd. "There you are." She bustled toward us, her long, polka-dotted black dress flowing around her and a tissue clutched in each hand. "I've been looking all over for you two."

You two, she'd said. Were we some kind of joined unit now? I supposed so given that we'd eaten peach cobbler and committed a crime together.

"I have news about the AGs," Gran continued, almost out of breath. "I told them all about you, and they want to meet you, Victoria."

It took forever for my mind to catch up with what she was talking about. Our finding-me-a-coven discussion seemed like weeks ago. The AGs, or the Anything Goes, wanted to meet *me*?

"They'll come to your home tonight at seven," she said.

"*Tonight*? Wait, they're coming to Sunray's?"

She nodded. "They say the best way to get to know a witch is meeting them while surrounded with the things that matter to them."

"But tonight's so soon." I wasn't ready. Not even a little bit.

"There's no need to impress them. All they're interested in is you. Just be yourself, and I'm sure they'll welcome you into their"—she mouthed the word "coven" as more people swept toward the exit gates—"with open arms."

"Just remember their name, the Attorney Generals," Travis told me. "I mean the Anything Goes." He grinned. "Anything, even you."

I wasn't so sure. After all, it took a certain kind of special to blow up half a block with magic.

Chapter Eleven
Anything Goes

Nothing could've prepared me for the explosion of satin and frills and floral perfume marching through my apartment door at seven o'clock sharp. The Anything Goes were five women ranging in age from twenties to fifties. They wore matching dresses in different pastel colors. As I held open the door for them, they ignored me and my false smile. I hadn't even invited them in.

"Victoria Fox, I presume," the one with the pastel purple dress said.

"That's me." Slowly, I closed the door, forcing myself not to flee through it first. I even locked it so I'd stay put. Recently, though, locking this door was a struggle. The lock practically ripped off my fingers to get it to engage. I groaned as it finally slid into place.

The Anything Goes frowned at the noise and at my apartment. Their magic radiated from them and shrank the living room to the size of a coffin. The one with the purple dress traced her finger over The Place To Put Things I Don't Want To Think About Today, otherwise known as the kitchen table where my grimoire and college application lay. She flicked the thick layer of dust on her skin with a disgusted grimace.

"I'm Aster Perkins, High Priestess of the AGs," she said. "This is Poinsettia, Abrus, Oleander, and Drosera."

Each of the witch's heads bobbed in turn at the introduction, just like the deadly plants and flowers they were named after. The air evaporated from my lungs. What kind of magic did these witches do?

"This isn't the entire coven, but it will be enough for you." She sniffed. "*What* is that smell?"

"Um, my familiar made a triple layer strawberry cake with cream cheese frosting." He'd gone out of his way to score points for me, though right now, he was nowhere to be found. I pointed at the impressive beauty of a dessert on the kitchen countertop, but no one even looked in that direction.

"No, the other smell," Aster said, her whole face scrunched like she'd eaten something sour.

Was it my apartment? Me? But I'd put on an extra layer of deodorant just for them.

"It smells like..." She sniffed again. "*Car.*"

"Oh, that must be my shop downstairs." When they all looked at me with blank expressions, I tried to clarify. "Sunray's Auto Shop. I'm a mechanic."

Aster's jaw dropped. "How awful."

An angry flush burned up my neck to my cheeks. "Not if you have a car that's broken down."

"I don't," she snipped.

Well. Okay, then.

"Aren't you going to invite us to sit?" Pastel Pink asked. Was that Oleander or Poinsettia? I couldn't remember.

"Ew," Pastel Yellow muttered. She made a face at the couch and chairs and held her hands to her chest as though something might fly up and crunch on her.

My flush raced to the tips of my ears, and I gritted my teeth. My apartment wasn't *that* bad. "Please. Take a seat wherever you like."

They did, their satin dresses sighing as one. I plunked down on the window seat a little too hard, sending up a large dust mote. Just then with a dramatic pop, Studmuffin appeared right next to me.

I yelped and nearly flung myself off the cushion to the floor. "Don't do that," I hissed, clutching my chest over my galloping heart.

As usual, he ignored me and gazed at our guests with his judgmental, you-just-missed-your-final-exam stare.

They stared right back, clearly unimpressed.

Aster clicked her tongue. "Your familiar, I presume."

Nodding, I attempted to smooth the wrinkles from my funeral dress I hadn't bothered to change out of. "Professor Studmuffin Salvitore III. He makes calorie-free desserts that look prettier than those in magazines and causes trouble." I frowned down at him. "Those are his main talents."

"He?" Aster leaned forward on the couch. "Did you say your familiar is a...*male*?"

"Well...yeah. He's a he. Why?"

She sat up straight again, her lips puckered in that sour twist again. "Witches have familiars of the *same* gender. That's how it's always been."

"Are you sure he's a familiar and not some street cat?" Pastel Pink asked.

"He just appeared next to me. Did you not just see that? Plus, he made that cake right over there." I pointed. Still, no one looked. "But yes, he also came off the street and into my shop one day five months ago."

The five of them shared a look.

Frowning, Aster clasped her hands in her lap. "So he *is* a street cat. A familiar cat who came in off the street."

Why on earth was that a bad thing? The hair bristled along my arms at the same rate it did along Studmuffin's spine.

I put my arm around him defensively. "He's my familiar. He's mine, and I don't plan on trading him in just because he's the wrong gender and came in off the street."

Aster gave me a long, withering look then snapped her fingers at Pastel Orange. "Abrus, why aren't you taking notes?"

"*Oh.*" Pastel Orange whipped out a notebook and an orange pen with a huge dangly puffball at the end.

Studmuffin crouched and tensed, prepared to put those murder mittens of his to use. Good thing I still had my arm around him to hold him back.

Aster turned to me again. "I noticed your grimoire on your kitchen table. What's your favorite spell?"

Ah, here we go. Now to really impress them with my lack of skills. "I'm, uh, between favorite spells at the moment. I haven't done much magic lately."

Pastel Orange wrote in a flurry, making the puffball swing and dance and tease my poor familiar. Studmuffin twitched and clacked. I tightened my hold on him.

"What's the last spell you did and when?" Aster asked.

"A summoning spell. Senior year in high school, so seventeen years ago." I cleared my throat and shifted my feet. I was afraid they would ask for specifics, and I was right.

"To summon whom?" Aster pressed.

"My...my mom. She left after I was born." Whenever I talked about her, which was very rare, my heart raced and broke all at once. It was like it was trying to run away from the hurt, but couldn't. I tried not to let it show on my face.

Aster nodded slowly. "So the summoning spell wasn't successful?"

"It was not."

"Why? What happened?"

I sighed, mentally readying myself for their judgement. "I misread the word now. I thought the grimoire said won, and I blew up half the street, nearly taking Sunray's with it. I'm dyslexic, you see. I have been my whole life."

The room went still. Even Pastel Orange's pen scratches stopped as they all stared.

I stared right back, feeling my cheeks flame. Studmuffin flicked his tail into my back repeatedly as if to pat it and offer comfort.

"We would like to see your broom," Aster finally said.

"My..." I pointed at the broom closet by the front door where I kept my vacuum. "Oh, *that* kind of broom."

"Yes, Victoria. *That* kind of broom." Aster lifted her eyebrows. "Or are you between brooms at the moment as well?"

I squeezed my hands into fists. "Yeah, I don't have one of those. I've never had one. I drive a car named Bernadette."

Pastel Orange wrote all of this down. Studmuffin clacked frantically at her pen. The rest of the Anything Goes looked ready to fall asleep, except Aster. Her face was so scrunched up I thought for sure her upper lip would get sucked right into her nose.

"Do you know any other witches?" she asked.

"No. I mean, my mom was supposedly a witch, but..." I frowned. "Why is this relevant?"

Aster ticked the answers off on her fingers. "You don't do magic. You don't own a broom. You don't know any witches. After all this time, what made you decide you wanted to join a coven right now?"

I opened my mouth then closed it. I hadn't thought there'd be such hard questions designed to deep-dive into my sugar-rattled brain. Like I always did, though, I answered honestly.

"Next to my grimoire," I started, "you might've seen a dusty manila envelope from the University of Georgia. It's an application, unopened, never filled out. It's been there for eighteen years now. Recently, I had an offer to buy Speedy Zone across town and run it, but I turned the offer down. Some may not need a business degree to run not one, but two businesses, but I feel that I do. Boxy co-manages Sunray's with me, but like he reminded me today at Jake's funeral, he won't be around forever. I guess the offer to buy Speedy Zone crumbled my resistance to college a little, made me wonder if I really could be a proper businesswoman. Since the application is lying right next to my grimoire, it made me wonder about that too."

"What or who is this *Boxy*?" Aster asked.

"He just goes by Boxy," I said. "He's a delightful, one-eyed ninja."

The room filled with a heavy silence and a whole lot of stares.

"From what it sounds like," Aster began, "Boxy is also a male"—big frown—"but do you have any girlfriends? Friends who are girls you go out to tea with or who you confide in?"

"Uh, no." Once again, I wondered how this was relevant. "I don't go out to tea with anyone. I had some girlfriends in high school, but as soon as we graduated, they moved away."

Aster nodded slowly. "Other than Boxy and your familiar, you're all alone, then."

"Well, no, because I do have them." Where was she going with all these questions?

"What would you do if Boxy left?"

"I— He wouldn't."

Aster's eyebrows flew up her forehead. "We all leave, in one way or another, Victoria. How would you cope?"

By not answering that question. "Okay, I see your point, but what does this have to do with me joining your coven?"

Aster smiled, but there was nothing friendly about it. "Tell me, is a witch who doesn't do magic really a witch?"

"You're the second person to ask me that in less than twenty-four hours." I heaved a sigh. This seemed to be going *so* well. "I still have magic in me. In high school, I successfully levitated for ten whole minutes. Freaked my dad out, but..." I shrugged. "I know I can do it."

Aster looked doubtful. "Do you think you can do a proper summoning spell if you try again?"

I glanced over at my grimoire and swallowed thickly. Pastel Orange hovered her pen over her notebook, waiting. Studmuffin remained locked on the dangly puffball.

"Um, I'm not sure I have the courage to do that at this point," I finally admitted.

"Do you think you could succeed at the University of Georgia?" Aster asked.

My eyes started to sting, and I wasn't sure exactly why. I'd never needed to prove myself, but now I found myself trying to do it again and again. Prove my innocence. Prove I was worthy of this coven. Prove my dyslexia couldn't stand in my way of being a savvy businesswoman.

"I don't know." My voice cracked a little. "I've never tried college before."

Aster smoothed her purple satin dress. "There are alternatives, you know. Acceptance into a coven provides opportunities for scholarships to various witch colleges. You could get a degree in everything from cosmic witchcraft to potions. The five of us have degrees in—"

"Earth witchcraft?"

She nodded. "Very good."

It was hardly a leap given the AG's poisonous plant names. "Cars and this shop are what I know. I can't imagine doing anything different or putting a degree like potions to use."

Aster tsk-ed. "Yet if you don't do something different, everything stays the same, doesn't it?"

Hmm, was that intended to be helpful or a diss? Either way, she might be right. I was like a puddle of stagnant water, unmoving, unchanging, often oily, and sometimes a little bit stinky. Did I want to be something else though?

Aster stood. "We'll be in touch, Victoria."

The rest of them rose from their seats and swept toward the door in a hurry.

"Wait, I don't get to ask you any questions?" I called to them.

Slowly, they turned to face me.

"What else could you possibly want to know?" Aster asked.

Um, everything? They hadn't shared a single thing about how they operate. Were there coven membership dues? (I could pay in loose change). Were there blood rites? (No thanks). What kind of frothy drinks were served at the summer solstice? (Glittery pineapple, please). Was ugly pastel a required color of all members? (Hard pass).

"Why call yourselves Anything Goes if nothing does?" I blurted.

Aster advanced toward me, a towering figure since I still sat on the window seat. Her power surrounded me, suffocated me.

Studmuffin climbed into my lap as if to block an attack. His fur bristled, and a low growl rumbled from his throat. I scooped him up and stood to face her, two against one. Well, two against five. Not great odds at all.

By the door, Pastel Orange was scribbling furiously.

Aster stopped in front of me, too close, and crossed her arms. Something told me she wasn't used to being questioned or challenged in any way. "Anything *does* go, as long as it's approved by me first."

"And if it isn't?" I asked. "If someone in your coven does something of their own free will?"

"Then there is no coven for them to return to," she said through gritted teeth.

"You don't see the flaws in that? How can you possibly control every little thing?"

"I've been managing quite well for longer than you've not done any magic." She clicked her tongue and turned. "We'll be in touch."

"I have more questions though."

"No," she said on her way to the door. "You don't."

With a loud pop, Studmuffin disappeared from my arms. He reappeared on the back of the couch and swiped Pastel Orange's pen so the puffball flew directly into his mouth. He grinned, the pen part dangling in front of him. To top off his flawless steal, he struck his power pose. A murderous gleam flashed in his narrowed yellow-green eyes.

"What are you doing?" Pastel Orange screeched. "Give that back."

Aster fixed me with a glare over her shoulder. "Can you control your familiar?"

"No." I grinned, crossing my arms. "I can't." I wouldn't want to even if I could.

Muttering under her breath, Aster marched out, the other four trailing after her like trained puppies. On her way out, Pastel Orange looked back at Studmuffin and pouted.

When they were finally gone, Studmuffin played with the puff for hours. At least he got something out of the AGs' visit. All I got was most of the triple layer strawberry cake with cream cheese frosting.

Poor, poor me.

Chapter Twelve
Circling Sharks

BEFORE I COULD GO to Kole's Krafty Keys the next morning—before I could do anything really—we had our first customer in three full days. A woman with long black hair waited outside before we'd even officially opened. Next to her sat a sea-green Pinto with black and white racing stripes and a very flat tire.

I nearly kissed the pavement in my rush to open the garage doors and greet her. A customer! Hopefully a paying one! Thank you, car gods!

"We're open and we have tires and it won't take long at all to change it. We have payment plans and also take credit cards, checks, cash, or wampum. Just kidding on that last one." I thrust my hand toward her, well aware I was talking a mile a minute. "I'm Victoria Fox."

She grinned so hard her big brown eyes crinkled at the corners. "Cass Rudio." She shook my hand with a light grip, probably because three fingers on her right hand were bandaged.

She wore a long, off-white bohemian skirt with little tassels at the bottom paired with a tan-striped top. She must've had an exploding mustard situation recently because small yellow stains speckled her clothes and sandals. She looked about my age, maybe a little younger.

"Is Cass short for Cassandra?" I asked.

"It's short for Casserole," she said matter-of-factly.

No explanation, no change to her innocent expression. Just Casserole. I liked her already.

"Well, Cass, I hope you didn't hurt yourself trying to change your tire," I said, gesturing to her bandaged hand.

Her shoulders sagged, her whole being seeming to crush in on itself. "I'll tell you all about my other seven fingers if you want. But those three..." She shook her head solemnly. "I don't talk about those."

Okay, that was nearing piñata-at-a-funeral odd. It kind of sounded like her fingers were separate, trouble-making things from the rest of her. Surely there was a horror movie about that I hadn't yet seen. Hollywood, have your people call my people, and we'll do lunch so I can share that idea. If, you know, I had people.

"Fair enough." I jerked my head toward the shop. "Come on in to the waiting area. We have cake."

"Cake for breakfast?"

"Cake any time," I said. "There are no rules here."

She laughed as she followed me inside through the open garage. "The flat happened just as I got into town, sort of like a bad omen. I'm half tempted to leave as soon as it's fixed."

I bit down hard on my tongue. There'd been a murder within the last week and I was a suspect, but yeah, I wasn't going to agree with her bad-omen idea. Not while she was here to get her tire fixed anyway.

"Belle's Cove isn't terrible," I said. "There are lots of great little shops and diners on Main Street."

"And your shop, Sunray's. What a delightful name. I saw your sign in the nick of time."

"See? Not a bad omen, but a ray of sun. I'll get you fixed up in no time." I opened the door to the waiting area, noting that Studmuffin had already been hard at work. A blueberry lemon trifle topped with whipped cream lay on the counter next to sparkly-clean plates and forks.

"Oh, you have a familiar," Cass said, her voice rising with excitement. "I've always wanted one."

"What?" I looked around, but he wasn't even in here. "How do you know that?"

"He's sitting right there." She pointed to an empty chair at one of the little tables. "A handsome black and white cat, right? Named Professor Studmuffin Salvitore III? Love the name, by the way."

"But..." I blinked at her, totally lost. "How do you know that?"

She pointed at the chair again. "He just introduced himself to me."

"Ah, of course he talks to *you*." Shaking my head, I posted my hands on my hips. "He doesn't talk to me, though, and apparently he's doing a magic trick I've literally never seen before. Why is he like this?"

Cass settled herself into the chair opposite my invisible familiar. "Ohhhh, I see..."

I looked between her and the empty chair. "What does that mean?"

"I sometimes see people's future ghosts. Plants, people, animals, and apparently familiars. It's hard to tell them apart from their ghostly versions since they appear solid to me. They run into me all the time." She shrugged as if all of this was completely normal. "Or I run into them. Sometimes they run into each other, the live version and their future ghost. That is a wild time, let me tell you."

I fell into a chair at a table next to hers even though I don't remember doing so. "Future ghosts?"

"Yep."

"It's not like a deadly premonition, is it?" I swallowed hard as I glanced at the spot where ghostly Studmuffin sat. If I ever lost him, I didn't know what I would do. "*Is* it?"

"No, not at all." She reached her hand toward me as if to put me at ease. Little mustard dots—or what I thought was mustard—speckled her arm as well. "So, think of time more like a scribble than a straight line. It folds into itself and circles back, which means ghosts can haunt their living selves. They do it all the time, but it's usually innocent fun. They can also just hang out and relive the good old days while their living version lives out their normal days. Make sense?"

"Um." There was so much info packed into what she'd just said that time would scribble itself out before I could unravel all of it. "So you can see ghosts?"

She nodded. "I can."

"Can you talk to the recently deceased?" I asked hopefully.

"Sorry, I can't." Her face fell. "I mean I've tried with like séances and stuff, but I've never had any luck with that. For some reason, the living version has to be nearby for me to see and hear the ghost. It's like they're still connected, or something. It would be so cool if I could speak to the recently departed though. Who would you want me to talk to?"

"Just a friend." I shrugged as if it was no big deal, but really, that would solve Jake's murder mystery in a heartbeat.

Jake, who killed you?

Oh, it was so-and-so because something wasn't there when the candle burned.

Boom, case closed.

"If you can see ghosts, then that makes you a—"

"Witch, but with a lowercase w," she said with a nod. "I'm still small-time. I'm actually here to see if I can find a coven that won't kick me out. And one that isn't too crazy."

"Oh, I didn't know you can get kicked out of covens." Of course, to get kicked out, one would need to accept me into the coven first, wouldn't they?

She glanced down at her three bandaged fingers as though they'd gone rogue and might've had something to do with it. "Do you happen to know of any covens around here that are accepting new members?"

"I'm trying to find one myself," I said with a sigh. "It'd be easier if they showed up on your doorstep and recruited you, but I guess that's not how it works."

"It does work that way *if* you're good."

"Ah, well, that explains it. I'm not very good," I admitted. Call it witch intuition, but I didn't think she was the judgy type, so I continued. "I blew up half of this block once with a summoning spell."

She winced and then it morphed into shock. "How does a summoning spell blow things up?"

"I read a word wrong from my grimoire, and things just kind of, uh, blew up from there."

Out the window behind Cass's head, a police car was creeping past. It had almost derailed my train of thought. It was probably nothing though.

"Sorry," Cass said sheepishly.

"Eh." I waved it off. I'd talked about it too much over the past few days, and each time I did, a new hot-cold dose of guilt swamped my gut. So I changed the subject. "Yesterday I had an interrogation with the AGs, or the Anything Goes. They're a coven here in town. I should warn you, though, that anything does *not* go. Nothing goes, in fact."

"That bad, huh?" She groaned and shook her head. "I think I'll avoid them. I've heard there are others in town though."

Another cop car rumbled slowly past. A sense of dread iced up my back. Was this a test of some kind? Were they trying to see if I'd panic and run?

"Does your familiar always look at you like that?" Cass asked.

"Hm? Like what?" I asked, pulling my gaze away from the window.

The live version of Studmuffin strode in then from the stairs, ignoring the both of us and heading straight for the ghost in the chair.

"He's got the most adoring smile on his face when he looks at you." She laughed as she watched both versions of my familiar. "Not the real one. He looks like everyone forgot to study, but the ghost of him... He must have really fond memories of you."

Despite the circling sharks outside, my chest warmed. "We're inseparable, even if I didn't study for his test. He's my little fluffer-stinker."

Studmuffin looked over his shoulder at me and scowled at the nickname.

I scowled right back, but it didn't last long before I broke into a grin. "Fluffer. Stinker."

Chuckling, Cass shook her head. "You two have given me witch familiar life goals."

"We're quite a pair," I said, glancing out the window again.

Boxy was just now pulling in, a deep frown on his face and his gaze stuck to the rearview mirror. I bet he knew something was wrong too. I just hoped he knew *what* was wrong.

Studmuffin flicked his tail then leaped up onto the chair next to his ghost. They seemed to bump noses, though it was hard to tell, and began purring loudly.

"Aw, he loves himself. That almost never happens. Usually it's chaos and screams." With a broad smile, Cass clasped her hands together, careful of her three bandaged fingers. But her smile froze when her gaze snagged on the window behind her. "There sure are a lot of cops here. Do they always drive so slowly?"

"They're just, uh, very protective of the town." I popped up out of my seat. "I should get going on your tire."

Before they stopped and arrested me. Had something changed in the case to make them really focus on me? Other than me entering Jake's house, minus the breaking? Because they couldn't know about that. Could they?

"Help yourself to some blueberry lemon trifle," I told Cass.

I hurried through the side door and shared a look with Boxy as he entered the garage.

"What's going on?" he asked, a V forming between his eyebrows.

"I wish I knew."

"Who's she?" He jerked his chin toward the waiting area door. Through the postage-stamp windows, Cass was cramming a large bite of trifle into her mouth. "Maybe they're looking for her."

"Chances are they're looking for me." My stomach sank at the three cop cars pulling into the parking lot. "I'm not all that hard to find."

The officers climbed out of their cars. One of them was Detective Palmer.

Boxy flipped up his cane in front of me as if to protect me with his secret ninja skills or make me disappear. I could only wish for that.

"What's this all about?" Boxy asked them as they came in.

Ignoring him, Detective Palmer held up a stack of official-looking papers. "Victoria Fox, we have a warrant to search your premises."

"Why?" I squeezed out, my voice sounding like I was breathing through a straw.

He shook the papers, his steely gaze raking over my face. "We have probable cause to believe you were involved in the murder of Jake Williams."

Chapter Thirteen

The Importance of Cat Glitter

"I WOULD NEVER KILL..." The garage began to tilt, and I slid down the decline.

Two hands and a paw reached out to steady me though. The officers and Detective Palmer spread into the garage, into the waiting area, and up the stairs into my apartment.

As soon as I was settled into a metal folding chair, Boxy whipped out his cell. "I'm calling my lawyer."

On my other side stood Cass who gently rubbed my back. It was the kindest thing a stranger had ever done for me. Studmuffin sat on my lap with both paws on my cheeks to absorb my tears. He always did that when I was sick or upset about something, my very own face-hugging therapist. I squeezed his warm body closer, and he nuzzled my nose.

"Remember to breathe," Cass was telling me. "I thought I was having a rough day, but I'm afraid you've got me beat. Is there anything I can do for you?"

I shook my head. "I still need to fix your tire."

"You let me worry about that," Boxy told me, still on the phone with his lawyer.

Lawyers. Search warrants. How had things gone off the rails so quickly? How could anyone think I was capable of murder when all I really wanted to do was fix cars and eat desserts and think about cracking open my grimoire again eventually?

Detective Palmer circled back through the waiting area and into the garage.

Boxy caned his way toward him faster than I'd ever seen him move. "Let me see that warrant."

The detective handed it over without breaking stride on a direct path toward me. "Ms. Fox, where were you Monday night?"

"Don't answer that," Boxy said, wagging his finger. "My lawyer said not to say a word until he gets here."

I crashed my back teeth together hard to keep from answering, not like I could with Studmuffin velcroed to my face.

Two nights ago, I was... Oh. Oh *no*. I was running into a house that wasn't mine on the furry heels of my familiar and then getting carpet burns on my hands and knees so I wouldn't get caught. Had Travis told?

Are we really doing this? I'd asked him.

When one door closes, another opens, he said. *That seems pretty relevant right now.*

Travis had been eager to go inside, but protective and kind of sweet and—

I noticed an eight-by-ten photo in the detective's hands.

Travis had also been armed with a cell phone to take pictures of me.

Detective Palmer held up the photo. In it, my gaze was immediately drawn to the bright, familiar yellow jacket someone wore while standing outside a house at night.

"Do you recognize this person?" he asked.

"No," I admitted, and got a mouthful of Studmuffin's neck when I did.

"No speaking, Vic," Boxy hissed. "Wait for the lawyer."

"Look again." Detective Palmer moved the photo so it fluttered into the back of Studmuffin's head. "Closer."

I folded back my familiar's ears and gently tried to stuff down his head, but he would not budge from my face. Still, I could kind of make out a few more details about the house in the photo, including the seashell wind chimes by the front door.

I gasped. "Jake's house."

"*Victoria*," Boxy warned, "I know where the duct tape is. Don't make me get it. Boro Yate will be here any minute."

Boro Yate, the lawyer. The same one written on Jake's calendar at his house. Boxy knew him?

Whoa, one seatbelt-free rollercoaster at a time.

I looked closer at the photo and found a date and time stamp at the bottom. Monday, June 20, 11:59 p.m. The same night I was at Jake's house but after I'd already left. The figure wearing the yellow jacket looked like a she with long turquoise hair pulled up into a ponytail, long tan legs in plaid shorts, and work boots. From the way that she was turned, I could almost see her front as she glanced left, but her face was a blur. Below the jacket, a familiar collar poked out. Underneath, it read su Ay to p.

Sunray's Auto Shop. That was *my* work shirt. She was dressed like me.

"But that's not me," I blurted.

Detective Palmer raised a skeptical eyebrow. "So it's someone who looks like you? Someone who broke Jake's lock to his home and went on in?"

"I'm not dumb enough to wear bright yellow when breaking and entering." Even I knew that, and I was only an expert at the entering part. "Besides, I don't know the first thing about breaking locks. What'd she use? A crowbar? Because I don't see her carrying one."

"Found it." A police officer walked into the garage from the waiting area with a bright yellow jacket hanging from the end of his flashlight in front of him.

"What do you mean you found it?" Boxy demanded. "Found what where?"

"Upstairs in the apartment," the officer said.

I popped up out of my chair, Studmuffin still clinging to me with his arms sliding down around my neck. "That's not mine. I've never owned anything like it."

Detective Palmer turned to me. "Ms. Fox, you were at Speedy Zone, the scene of Jake's murder, last week. Multiple witnesses say they saw someone wearing a yellow jacket run out the back door of Speedy Zone around the time the murder happened."

"Yes, I was one those witnesses, remember?" I said. "I saw the person in yellow, but it wasn't me."

"Then how do you explain the yellow jacket in your possession and the photo outside Jake's house of someone with your physicality wearing a Sunray's Auto Shop shirt?" the detective asked.

"I can't explain it. Someone must've broken into my apartment to steal one of my shirts and plant the jacket." But who? And when?

Boxy rubbed his hand down his chin and shook his head. "Vic, I hate to say it, but it sounds like someone's trying to frame you."

My head started to spin as though I'd stood too fast, but really, it was the idea that struck too hard.

The Anything Goes are dying to meet you, Gran had told me. *They say it has to be tonight at seven.*

Could one of the coven members have planted the jacket while they were here? But the photo in Detective Palmer's hand was taken Monday night. The Anything Goes were here on Wednesday. So, someone would've had to have broken into my apartment *before or during* Monday night to steal one of my work shirts.

Like while Studmuffin and I went to Jake's house with Travis. What a perfect opportunity to break into my apartment while I entered someone else's home. And who knew I'd be gone that night? Travis. Who'd set up the meeting with the Anything Goes on Wednesday? Gran Black. Were they pulling the strings of this entire investigation to put the blame on me and wipe out Sunray's for good?

How was business today? I'd asked Travis the night we went to Jake's.

A little slow but good, he'd said.

My business wasn't good. It really wouldn't be if I got thrown in jail.

"Were you at Jake's house Monday night?" Detective Palmer asked.

How to answer that? I wasn't so sure answering truthfully would shed the best possible light on me. In this particular moment, good lighting meant everything. I decided on telling a related truth that skirted around his question.

"Travis Black had the idea to walk to the wildlife refuge and see the sunset over the duck pond that evening." Technically true, even though we hadn't actually done that. I felt Boxy's gaze bore into me. Something told me I'd have to survive his inquisition, too, if I survived this one. "We met at Gas, Guzzle, & Go because he kept going on and on about their sushi. I passed on that."

"Smart thinking," one of the officers nearby muttered.

"What time was that?" Detective Palmer asked.

"About eight thirty. After the wildlife refuge, I came home about ten." Then it hit me. "*That* was when I noticed the lock on my door was harder to lock."

That night had to have been when someone broke inside. Had Travis wanted me to see the wildlife refuge because it would keep me away from my apartment even longer?

The detective waved a policeman upstairs, presumable to check out the lock. "*If* someone broke in, stole one of your work shirts, and planted the jacket here, who might have done it?"

Well, to answer that, I'd have to be honest with myself first. I had zero chances of ever getting accepted into the Anything Goes. Even if they welcomed me with open arms, I already knew they weren't for me. Now, that didn't mean I wanted to throw them under the proverbial bus, but no one else had been in my apartment since then other than Studmuffin and me. That I knew of anyway.

"A...group of women came over after Jake's funeral." I winced inwardly, unsure how much Detective Palmer knew about witches and covens.

"Who?"

"Aster Perkins and four others with poisonous plant names."

He nodded as though he knew who I was talking about.

Just then, a black BMW pulled into the parking lot. A portly man in a fancy blue suit hopped out. The lawyer from the commercials was here. Boro Yate than never.

"Not another word. Not another word," he said in a thick Georgia accent to no one in particular.

While he read over the search warrant, Boxy filled him in on the latest.

Cass floated up behind the officer who still held the yellow jacket and squinted at it for a moment. "I think Victoria can prove this jacket isn't hers."

"Of course I can," I said absently, but I had no idea how.

She pointed to Studmuffin, and then all the rest of Studmuffin clinging to my clothes and face. Cat glitter, aka cat fur.

"I *can*," I said, almost triumphantly. "Look at me. I'm covered in cat fur, and I shed almost as bad as he does. Between the two of us, we could make blankets for the entire state of Georgia, if, you know, that was a thing people and cats did." I cleared my throat. Now was *not* the time to be weird. "That jacket though?" I shook my head. "There isn't any human or cat fur on it that I can see."

"And it's cotton, which is a magnet for hair and fur," Cass added.

The officer holding the jacket frowned as he examined the fabric closer. "She's right. I don't see anything."

Boxy hobbled toward the jacket while wagging his finger in the air. "I know all about hair despite not having much. One time I went home from Sunray's feeling like something was squeezing my big toe. Come to find out it was one of Vic's long turquoise hairs that had worked its way into both my shoe *and* my sock and wrapped itself around my toe like some kind of friendly, hairy python."

"Sorry, Boxy." I turned to the detective who had his arms crossed and was rubbing his jaw thoughtfully. "Even if I had the jacket dry-cleaned, which I didn't because it's not mine, I still don't think I would've gotten all the fur and hair off if I'd worn it."

The policeman the detective had sent upstairs to check the lock came back into the garage. "I found some scratch marks on the apartment door's lock that suggests someone picked it. I tried to take fingerprints from it, but it's been wiped clean."

"That settles it, then." Boro Yate clapped his hands and made everyone but the detective jump. "We're done for today. My client's lock has been tampered with, and she says the jacket isn't hers. If you can find one shred of DNA evidence that says the jacket really is hers, then and only then will you have a case against her that will stand up in court. Your blurry photograph sure won't do it. While we await the results of your findings, my client will behave herself and stay in Belle's Cove. Until then, good day to you, Detective." With that, he saluted me, shook Boxy's hand, and strode quickly away to his BMW.

At the detective's nod, the officers slowly began to disperse, even the one with the yellow jacket.

He bagged it up in a large plastic bag that read Evidence.

"I'll be in touch, Victoria," Detective Palmer told me and then strode away to the police cars out front.

I sat in stunned silence while Boxy and Cass talked excitedly, but I couldn't pay attention. Studmuffin pulled away and looked up at me as if he wasn't quite sure what to do with himself. I felt the exact same way.

One thing was certain though—now I had a fabulous reason to go to Kole's Krafty Keys and get a brand new, tamper-proof lock.

Chapter Fourteen

Killer

This time, I had a plan. Instead of asking rapid-fire questions like I had with Jake's fiancée, I would ease into it with Kole from Kole's Krafty Keys. Jake's fiancée had all but shut down and run away from me. I couldn't let that happen again. I needed answers, now more than ever.

But my plan fled out the window as soon as I walked into the store.

A puppy bounded after a ball straight for me, tongue wagging out the side of its mouth. Its huge feet skidded all over the waxed floor, failing to gain traction. It was so determined to get that ball, though, that it didn't even realize I'd stepped in its way. Before it could crash into me or spiral into orbit out the front door, I scooped it up. The puppy thanked me by slathering my face with kisses.

"Oh, yes, I love you too," I cooed.

Booming laughter echoed through the store. I looked up to see the man who'd let himself into Jake's to smash his candles. The man who'd almost caught Travis and me. Jake's uncle, Kole. Instead of a red vest, he wore a snazzy blue one with jeans.

His belly shook when he laughed and his cheeks turned rosy. That definitely lessened any murderer vibe, but these days, I didn't trust anyone. Still, it was hard to think about murder while holding an adorable, wiggly puppy.

It had huge, floppy ears and oversized paws for its little white-spotted body. Pair those things with big, innocent green eyes, and I was a goner.

"He's just found his new best friend. Haven't you, boy. Haven't you?" Kole asked in that high-pitched voice reserved for talking to puppies. Then he turned to me. "Welcome to Kole's Krafty Keys."

"If this is how you greet your customers, I'll be coming every day, thanks," I said between chuckles and puppy licks.

The man laughed again, such a jovial sound. "Not a problem. Here, let me help you." He strode down the center aisle and gently took the sweet dog from my arms. "Other than offer you a towel for your face, what can I do for you today?"

"Well, for starters, I'm in need of a hearty new lock for my front door."

"Hearty, you say?" He frowned. "I hope there hasn't been any trouble."

"Nah, no trouble." I waved my hand, dismissing the very idea when really there'd been too *much* trouble. He didn't need to know that though.

"I've got just the lock," he said. "It includes a dead-bolt on the panel above the doorknob, which is included, and the whole thing is super sturdy. One second and I'll grab it."

He set the puppy down. Without anyone to love on, the puppy made a perfect O with his mouth and let loose a pitiful howl.

"Oh *no*," Kole and I said at the same time. Then we laughed and laughed.

I knelt in front of the devastated puppy and scooped him back up again. "Don't worry, I'll keep him company." And possibly kidnap him and take him home to Studmuffin who...

Yeah, never mind. My familiar had made it clear that I was to be owned by one animal and one animal only. Whenever anyone came to Sunray's with their pet or a fuzzy caterpillar inched into the garage or a butterfly fluttered in and landed on my shoulder, Studmuffin made it known I was *his*. Loudly. With people, he didn't have as much of a problem.

While Kole retrieved the lock from the back of the store, I entertained the puppy and searched for any signs that read Killer4Hire. Just kidding, sort of. I did look around though. This part of the store was spotless, with white floors polished to a high shine and framed posters on the walls. When I concentrated, the letters on one poster unscrambled themselves to promise "Key Kopies in Less Than 2 Minutes Guaran-Keyed!" Another read "Feeling Unlocky?" next to a woman standing by a car while pulling her hair out. Punny *and* funny. It was getting more and more difficult not to trust this guy.

"So, what we've got here is everything you need to install the new lock yourself," Kole said, striding to the front counter. "That way is the cheaper way, but if you'd rather, I can come and install it for you. I'll even give you a discount since my dog just about licked your face off." Chuckling, he waved a stack of paper towels at me from over the counter.

With one last pet on the puppy's head, I stood and took the towels just to be polite. "No worries. Puppy licks are great for the complexion, so I hear. What's his name?"

A sad, haunted shadow crossed the man's face. "My nephew called him Killer, but I can't bring myself to call him that."

Made perfect sense. Made more sense given the empty dog bowls at Jake's house. It also created a perfect opening for the other reason I was here. "Your nephew, Jake?"

"You know him?" He sighed and seemed to wilt a little. "*Knew* him?"

"We went to high school together. He was a good person. I'm really sorry about what happened to him."

He nodded, his chin trembling. "Taking care of his puppy is the only thing that's helping me get through this. My brother is devastated, and...I just wish I knew what happened and who could've done such a thing."

"You mentioned that you're taking care of the puppy now, but didn't Jake have a fiancée who lived with him?" I asked gently.

He snorted and shook his head. "Cherry Berenstein? She wishes. They were never even engaged. I don't even know for sure if they were ever dating, but she went around town telling everyone they were getting married. Jake wanted nothing to do with her."

Hm, then how did she have access to his house? That would explain why there wasn't more female stuff there though.

"Was he interested in someone else?" I asked.

He shrugged. "Could have been. Jake could have had his pick of anyone in Belle's Cove. Why, were you interested in him?"

"Uh, no, I just thought she lived with him. I happened to be on my way downtown when I saw a blonde come out of his house." I mean, it was sort of true. "I also saw her at the funeral standing next to the rest of Jake's family, so I just assumed they were really together."

"Her standing with us caused quite a ruckus with my brother, let me tell you. Cherry has a key to Jake's place. How she got it, I'll never know, but I went there a couple nights ago to change the locks and bolt the windows shut. When I got there, one window was wide open."

"You don't say..." It made sense that was what he was doing there. That, and breaking candles.

"She has absolutely no business being there," he continued, "and if she was there as you say, she must've left her crazy cat. I've never seen one climb the walls like that."

I hid my snort with a "Wow, that's awful" and an appropriate level of shock. Then I shuffled my feet because this next question would require some easing into. "So, I was talking to Gran a couple days ago... You know, Gran Black?"

"Peach cobbler," he declared, a brief, though triumphant smile on his face. He raised his fist for a bump.

I did, and we exploded our hands apart as I said, "No joke. Cobbler for the win every time."

"Gran is one of the friendliest people I've ever met," he said. "She's invited me over to her house for dinner so many times that I call it my second home."

"Nice." I cleared my throat. It hurt to think she might've had something to do with framing me for murder, but I would have to face that possibility later. "Anyway, we were eating cobbler and trying to understand how something like this could happen to Jake. She mentioned that she overheard him on his cell when he was on Main Street one day. He said something wasn't there when the candle burned. Does that mean anything to you?"

"Oh, that." Nodding, he tossed one of the balls on the carpeted counter to Not Killer who immediately flopped after it. "Yeah, he was talking to me."

I sucked in a breath, unsure what to do or say next after hearing that bit of news. For once, I kept quiet and hoped he'd continue on his own.

He watched Not Killer play for a moment with a sad, faraway expression in his eyes. Then, eventually he said, "Everyone loved Jake, but especially my mom, his grandmother. In her will, she left him an heirloom. When my mom's mom died, she left *her* an heirloom. It had been passed down again and again and had more sentimental value than any amount of money. Or so we thought. When Mom passed, she hid it in one of the candles she hand-poured. Mom's family was poor growing up, so to save on electricity, they made beeswax candles. When the candle was given to Jake, he burned it and discovered it was a normal beeswax candle. There was nothing inside."

Interesting place to hide something so valuable. It could've been a genius place if someone hadn't found the heirloom. "Your mom must've known it was valuable if she hid the heirloom inside a candle."

"Yeah, I think she must've had the heirloom appraised when she started her will. Or maybe she finally found out exactly what it was." He shrugged. "All I know is that Jake was awfully upset about the whole thing because he thought he'd lost it."

"Poor Jake," I murmured. "Could someone think that this heirloom was valuable enough to kill for?"

"It's hard to believe, but..." He smiled sadly at Not Killer who gnawed on his ball. "Maybe."

"What did this heirloom look like?" I asked.

Kole took a deep breath and then slowly released it. "It's a ring. I only saw it once when Mom wanted to see if it fit me. It didn't. It did fit Jake though. It's silver with a dark blue sphere no bigger than a marble suspended in the middle of tiny silver clouds."

Nodding, I bit down hard on my tongue on the question I wanted to ask next—did the ring glow? If so, I might have seen it before on a certain someone's finger.

Instead, I placed my hands on the counter, fingers spread open wide just like my soul was about to be. It was time for some major truth-telling. "Kole, I feel like I need to be honest with you. I was at Speedy Zone the night Jake was killed. The police questioned me, and just this morning, they had a warrant to search my shop."

Somehow, I kept my voice even and the tears held back, though I could definitely feel their sting. This morning's events were foggy in my mind, as if they'd happened to someone else, because they sure couldn't happen to me.

Kole just stared, his mouth hanging open.

"I believe someone found out I was there at Speedy Zone that night," I continued, "and now they're trying to place the blame on me. It's well-known that the Blacks and the Foxes have some bad blood between us, so I'm the easiest target. But I can assure you, I would *never* hurt Jake. If this heirloom is the reason he was killed, it's the first I'm hearing about it."

Some of the color had drained from Kole's face. He gazed down at Not Killer again and then blew out a slow, unsteady breath. "You say the police had a search warrant, but if you're standing here, they must not have found anything."

"They did, actually. My front-door lock that was tampered with and a yellow jacket that isn't mine. Detective Palmer got an anonymous tip and a photo of someone in front of Jake's house Monday night. Someone who looks a lot like me wearing my work shirt and that same yellow jacket I mentioned. The only reason I wasn't arrested is because the jacket didn't have a scrap of my hair or my cat's hair on it. And see?" I plucked off several hairs from my black shirt sleeve. "There's a lot."

Kole whistled low. "That's why you need a new lock."

"Exactly. Someone broke in to steal a work shirt and then broke in another time to plant the jacket."

"How do you know they broke in twice?" he asked, his forehead wrinkling.

I blinked. "Huh?"

"It would take some nerve to break in twice. If I were a criminal, I'd do it once so as not to leave a trail. Go in, steal the shirt, plant the jacket, get *another* jacket for the photo op."

I threw my head back and sighed. "Wow, you're right. If that's the case, then maybe the Anything Goes didn't have anything to do with it."

"The what now?" Kole asked.

"Never mind," I said, digging through my purse for my wallet. "Kole, you've been very helpful. To show my thanks, I'd love to pay full price for this lock. No puppy-licks discount required."

With a reluctant nod, he rang the lock up on the old-fashioned cash register. "I believe you, you know. You wouldn't hurt Jake."

I forced down the sudden lump in my throat as I paid him. "That means the world to me that you think so. Thank you. If you or any of Jake's family ever need your cars serviced, I'll give you a steep discount."

He bagged up the lock and handed it to me, a warm smile on his face. "We'd love to pay full price."

"Well, thanks again." I stooped down behind the counter to hide my misty eyes and to scratch the puppy behind the ears. "Goodbye, Not Killer. I'll come see you again soon."

"Take care now," Kole said when I stood to leave.

I waved, still seeing teary blurs, and fumbled my way out the door.

Outside, though the breeze warmed my wet cheeks, the hair at the back of my neck stood on end. I slowed my steps toward Bernadette parked at the curb, my pulse thumping wildly.

Someone was watching me.

I knew this before I saw them. When I flicked my gaze across the street, sure enough, someone leaned against a parked car, openly staring. Like me, they were dressed all in black to disguise themselves. With their sweatshirt hood drawn low over their shaded eyes, I couldn't tell if they were male or female. I didn't recognize the white Toyota Camry behind them. A *white* car... The same one Ms. Stevenson saw speeding away from Speedy Zone when her bookmobile died?

All of this I saw in an instant. Then I pivoted right, away from Bernadette, and headed down the sidewalk.

There I was, flaunting my freedom around town, while my framer—or framers—had expected me to be tossed in jail. I wanted to see what this person would try to do about it. I also wanted to see if I could circle back and catch the license plate number on the white Camry.

I glanced behind me.

Oh, good. Not only was I being watched, but now I was being followed.

Chapter Fifteen

Stop and Wave to the Dead Weeds

I WAS SO FOCUSED on my follower, I didn't even notice one of Main Street's shop doors opening. I plowed into it face-first, because of course I did, and nearly knocked the poor woman coming out of it right over. The plastic bag in her hand dropped and skidded across the sidewalk.

"Oh," I squeaked.

A pair of big brown eyes framed by long black hair met mine. "Victoria?"

"Cass," I whispered, "you shouldn't be here."

"At a drugstore? But I needed some biodegradable moist towelettes. Plus, they had the cutest polka-dotted gardening gloves. *On. Sale.* Ninety-nine cents, for not one glove, but *two*." She threw up her hands. "Can you even believe it?"

I hastily picked up her shopping bag, thrust it into her hands, hooked my elbow through hers, and booked it up the sidewalk with her. "No, I mean you shouldn't be here with *me*."

She blinked hard. "*You* ran into *me*."

"I know. I'm sorry. I mean you shouldn't be seen with me." I reached over and squeezed her shoulder, so thankful she was here, yet so worried I might've just put her in danger by even talking to her. "Someone's following me."

She drew in a sharp inhale, her mouth hanging open. Then she closed her eyes and murmured something so low and so fast that I couldn't hear her.

A sudden gust of wind kicked up from behind us. It seemed to gain strength as it swept up the street toward us and slammed into our backs. My hair billowed around my face. My black shirt ballooned outward. A cup flew out of a nearby trashcan and clattered down the gutter. People coming out of storefronts stopped to shield themselves with the doors as they looked up at the sky as though a storm was brewing.

I knew better. It had come from Cass.

She pulled me closer with our hooked elbows and sped our pace. "You're right. They smell like onions and ashes."

I jerked back in surprise. "How do you know that?"

She shrugged. "Take a sniff."

Sure enough, the air smelled sharp and burned at the same time, but I didn't know anyone who smelled like that. Of course, I didn't go around sniffing people either. Good thing Studmuffin wasn't here—he hated the smell of onions.

"I mean how do you know that's what the person who's following me smells like?" I asked. "It could be anything."

"I asked the earth if anyone nearby had bad intentions, and she told me." She pointed at herself with her bandaged hand. "Earth witch, remember? The person following you definitely has bad intentions."

Like a murderer usually would. This one wanted to announce those intentions loud and clear in broad daylight because I wasn't taking the blame for Jake's death so easily. They'd wanted me to see them and to know they were a threat.

My heart galloped into my throat. I'd never been anyone's target before, especially a murderer's.

"Are you thinking what I'm thinking?" Cass asked, her brows drawn together in concern.

"That we should have a foot race?" I said, my voice unsteady. "Most definitely."

We turned the corner at the next block, and then we broke into a run.

"Is this a typical day for you?" she asked, puffing as much as I was. "Police, search warrants, framed for murder, and now this?"

"Only lately." I threw a glance over my shoulder. All clear, so far.

We dodged right into an alleyway and ducked down behind a stack of cardboard boxes next to a dumpster. The smell back here completely suffocated any traces of onions and ashes.

"But I've been up to more shenanigans than usual," I continued, clutching the stitch in my side, "and I'm the instigator for a lot of this. I'm a shenanigator."

Cass doubled over laughing. "Stop. Don't make me laugh. Running hurts too much as it is."

"Sorry." I peered over the boxes. Along the sidewalk, a young mom pushed a stroller, but that was all. "Okay, come on. I want to circle around and take a photo of my secret admirer's car."

Cass was mid nod before her gaze strayed to the brick wall opposite us.

"What?" I asked. "Do you see something?"

"A ghost weed is visiting its living self. See that tall one there?" She pointed. "Its ghost is right next to it. Oh, she's waving."

We both waved back, Cass's much more enthusiastic than mine. Apparently I could only handle so much strange in one day. Waving to weeds, dead or alive, was off-the-charts strange.

Then, as fast as we could without running, we made our way to the other end of the alley. We tried to keep ourselves hidden behind more dumpsters and garbage piles and other stinky things I didn't want to look at too closely.

"I've always loved alleys, despite the smell," I admitted as I leaped over an oily puddle. "They're secret places easily forgotten, unless you happen to be in one. I used to stick to them on my way home from elementary school to avoid the bullies."

Cass grinned. "What a coincidence. I used to sneak down one behind a plant store I always went to. It had gardening gloves for sale, too, but never for ninety-nine cents. That's my dream, you know. Opening a plant store of my own. I'm going to call it I Just Wet My Plants."

Despite my day today, or maybe *because* of my day today, I burst into laughter. It swelled louder when Cass joined in, but thankfully, the growing sounds of traffic helped cover our snorts.

"That's the best store name I've ever heard," I said between gasps. "Please, can you just move to town right now and adopt me as your new best friend? If I ever get customers again, I'll send them all to I Just Wet My Plants."

She shrugged. "I'll see what the covens are like, but the more I'm here, the more I like the interesting people. I have to admit, I've never met anyone framed for murder who can change a tire in under five minutes before."

"What can I say? I'm a woman of many talents and twice as many failures. Speaking of which, will your store sell brooms by any chance? I was reminded by the Anything Goes that I don't have one."

"You mean a broom of the witchy variety?" she asked. "I can just make you one."

"Really?" I stared at her in shock.

"Of course," she said, grinning.

"That would be amazing. I— Wow. Just...wow. I mean thank you." Apparently I was so unused to kindness from people I'd forgotten how to speak. Being abandoned by my best customers and framed with murder would do that to you, I supposed.

Even in her long skirt, Cass easily jumped over a puddle. "You're welcome, but it's just a broom."

"It's not though," I told her as we turned out of the alley onto the sidewalk. "Almost everyone in town has turned their backs on me, so I guess it's hard for me to understand why you're being so nice."

"Because we're two witches who've had some hardships and are without covens." She leaned closer. "And if I'm being perfectly honest, your familiar's baking is outstanding. I want to make sure I stay in your good graces so he'll feed me more."

I laughed. "You're welcome back at Sunray's any time, whether you have a flat— There's the car! Quick, it's getting away."

Further up the street, past the intersection, the white Camry was headed away from us but stopped in traffic. Was it the same white Camry?

We raced to catch it. As we neared the traffic lights, I realized it very well could be the same one. The space where it had been parked before was empty.

My lungs burned. My breaths heaved. More stitches formed in my sides.

"Have I...mentioned...how much...I hate...running?" Cass squeezed out.

"Same." But I kept at it, fishing for my phone in my purse.

We neared the intersection. Somehow, the lights turned in our favor, and we sprinted across the street. Almost there. Almost close enough to get a picture of the license plate. The driver was nothing but a dark shadow behind the wheel.

Ten feet away. Still running, I lifted my phone to snap a picture.

Tires squealing, the car veered into oncoming traffic to the tune of many honking horns. Then it took an illegal left turn and sped away.

The driver must've seen me coming in the rearview mirror. The photo I'd gotten was nothing but a blur though.

"Bummer," I hissed between my teeth, but then I glanced up at the camera on the traffic light. "Maybe it got...something."

We collapsed against the building next to us to catch our breaths.

After a moment, Cass peered up at me. "Do your lungs or your legs or your heart hurt the worst?"

I groaned. "Yes."

Chapter Sixteen
Sweatpants Goblin

"HI, VICTORIA FOX CALLING for Detective Palmer, please."

A brief pause, then the female voice on the line said, "Right away, Ms. Fox."

I imagined the detective was pretty difficult to get ahold of unless you were a suspected murderer. So that's one happy positive, I guess.

It was late Thursday evening, and I was winding down this terrible day with my favorite feline already asleep in my lap. A little bit of cat drool had started to seep into my sweatpants. I didn't care though. This and his blueberry lemon trifle he'd baked earlier were exactly what I needed to relax and put some distance between myself and everything that had happened lately.

The lock on my door was now fixed, and every single window was closed and latched, which was rare for me. I preferred them open. After learning someone had invaded my private space, though, I wasn't taking any chances.

Except one. I'd invited Cass to stay the night since protection came easier in pairs, ignoring that whole stranger-danger thing just for her. We meshed well, I thought. She'd a found a motel next to a community garden though. That was for the best anyway, I supposed, since I turned into a sweatpants goblin after ten p.m. No offense to other sweatpants goblins out there, but I am of the lazier, grumpier variety.

Detective Palmer's gruff voice came over the line. "Ms. Fox, what a surprise."

"Have you found any of my hair or my cat's fur on that yellow jacket yet?"

"We just sent it off to the lab today," he said. "These things take time."

"Well, I may not have much of that left. I think whoever killed Jake is growing bolder. Someone was watching me today on Main Street and then followed me for a little ways. I doubt they were too happy I wasn't in jail."

A pen clicked. Something clattered, and then another pen clicked. "Can you describe them?"

"Not really. They were wearing sunglasses and all black, but they were leaning against a white Toyota Camry, which might be the same white car Ms. Stevenson saw behind Speedy Zone."

The detective scratched all of that down. "Did they say anything to you?"

"No. I was coming out of Kole's Krafty Keys to get a new door lock, and they were parked across the street. I think they wanted me to see them. They wanted me to feel uncomfortable, which yep, mission accomplished. I ran into a friend, and we cut through the alley and around to try to take a picture of their license plate."

"Are you sure all they wanted was to threaten you with their presence?"

"Well...no..."

"Maybe they wanted to scare you off. Were you parked in front of Kole's?"

"I was... You don't think they planted more evidence in my car, do you?" Poor Bernadette. She didn't deserve to be mixed up in all this.

"Anything is possible at this point, but if I were you, I would check."

"I didn't notice anything, but I'll check more thoroughly first thing tomorrow morning."

"Fine. You said you were trying to get a picture of the person's tags?"

"I tried but didn't get anything except a giant blur. That's part of why I'm calling though. They took a rather creative left turn at the corner of Main Street and Divine Avenue. Maybe the traffic light caught this person's tags?" My voice pitched higher with hope.

"I'll do some checking. What time was this?"

"About five thirty. And Detective, maybe you already know this, but Jake was missing an heirloom his grandmother gave him."

"I *am* aware." A note of irritation crept into his tone. He sure wasn't used to having his skills doubted, was he?

"I think if we find that, then we find the killer."

"There is no we in any of this, Ms. Fox," he said sternly, "but I agree."

"Do you know anything else about the heirloom? Why someone would think it's more valuable than Jake's life?"

A heavy pause, then, "I'm not at liberty to discuss those particular details of the case."

So he probably didn't know, either, but had hunches, same as me.

"Ms. Fox, I..." He drummed his pen—or what sounded like it—on his desk. "I need you to take care of yourself, okay?"

"Because you believe I'm not a murderer and wish the town hadn't sentenced my business to death before I was even arrested or charged?" I said in a rush.

He sighed. "Because I'm trying to look out for everyone in Belle's Cove. Talk soon, Ms. Fox." He hung up.

I hung up, too, and tapped my phone to my chin, considering what he'd just said. Would he be so worried about me if he thought I was guilty? Maybe the good old detective was coming around to my way of thinking. The innocent way of thinking.

Now to see if some of my thinking was right.

The problem was my grimoire was all the way across the room on top of The Place To Put Things I Don't Want To Think About Today. The other problem was I sat underneath a sleeping cat. If waking him was a felony, waking him while he was blessing my lap was treason according to the kitty commandments. After I accidentally woke him while in my lap once, he spent the whole night freefalling from who knows where right onto my head. I didn't sleep a wink.

Even so, he was just so cute all curled up on my lap in a crustacean with one paw over his eyes. But one time I'd risked it all to use the bathroom and broken the kitty commandments without waking him. I could do it again.

Oh-so-gently, one slow inch at a time, I slipped my hands underneath him, making a sort of throne for him with my arms.

One of his eyes cracked open the slightest bit.

I stopped, frozen.

With a grunt, he closed it again.

I blew out a relieved breath, careful not to blow it on him. As if moving through syrup, I stood with him in my arms, my bones and joints protesting because I was shifting sooooo slowly. Then I took a step. And another one.

The floor creaked under my feet.

I tensed.

His tail dangled over my arms and swatted at them once, twice, a clear warning.

Almost there. I kept going, faster this time, toward the kitchen table. Dread plunged to the bottom of my stomach as I drew closer. This must've been exactly how Frodo felt on his way to Mordor, if he'd been carrying a temperamental, sleepy cat as well as the ring.

Careful not to squeak the chair legs, I pulled out a chair with my foot, nearly stumbled, but didn't. Then, with a long sigh, I slid into the chair and laid Studmuffin on my lap again.

The things we do for our cats.

As I dragged my grimoire toward me, I tried not to think about what I was doing too much. Seventeen years of dust wafted off the cover and pages when I flipped it open to the index in the back. I willed myself not to cough and undo all the work I'd done just to sit at The Place To Put Things I Don't Want To Think About Today. The words and letters arranged themselves into gibberish, but after several minutes of concentration, I found what I was looking for.

Heirlooms, magical – p. 863.

That section of the book had several ornately drawn pictures of cursed rings, hexed brooches, and even one poodle figurine known for granting wishes. When I turned the page, I gasped. There it was, the ring Kole had described, the ring Jake was missing. A dark blue sphere no bigger than a marble suspended in the middle of tiny silver clouds. Above the picture, it read: *The Ring of Everlasting Night. Avoid at all costs.*

Oh. That didn't sound good.

Especially since it looked *just* like Travis and Gran Black's rings.

Chapter Seventeen
The Belly Up

"WHY DO I GET the feeling you're avoiding me?"

Without turning around, I clenched my teeth at the air filters I was doing inventory on for the sixteenth time since there was nothing else to do. It was He Who Only Comes Out at Night's voice on a bright and early Friday morning. Boxy wasn't even here yet.

"Probably because I'm avoiding you," I said.

Travis had sent a couple texts since the funeral, mostly about memorials for Jake and car memes. I'd ignored all of them.

Luckily his best friend, Studmuffin, was busy performing baking magic.

"I see..." Travis's frown trickled into his tone. "Mind telling me what I did wrong?"

"You can start by telling me about your ring," I demanded, still not facing him.

"It's...just a ring. Why do you ask?"

Why, indeed. How could he act so innocent when The Ring of Everlasting Night was attached to his finger?

I spun around. "Were you aware that Jake was missing a ring?"

His hazel eyes widened. "No, I wasn't aware. Do you think I'm a suspect now or something?"

"I guess it depends on if you're trying to frame me or not," I fired back.

His mouth popped open. "Why on earth would I ever try to frame you?"

"There were two people outside the back door of Speedy Zone that night, but who's to say there weren't more people in on it," I said, jabbing my finger at him. "And now you and your Gran are wearing rings just like the one Jake was missing."

He blinked hard. "I've been wearing this now for weeks. If Jake was missing one like it, don't you think he would've noticed I was wearing it? I guess this also means you suspect Gran now too. You know, there was a bank robbery about a year ago. I suppose you think we evolved from Bonny and Clyde to murderers, don't you?"

"Well," I began and crossed my arms, "you are members of the Black family."

A long, heavy silence followed, and I knew I'd pushed too far. There were so many things about Travis and Gran that didn't quite fit with Jake's murder, yet I couldn't ignore how secretive they were about their rings. Even now, he had both hands hidden behind his back.

"Ah, I get it." Travis nodded, his expression tight with hurt. "You're trying to push me away. You're afraid I'll get too close and then I'll leave."

His voice didn't trail off, but I heard the rest of what he didn't say plain as day. Just like my mom left. Just like all my friends in high school left. Just like dad. Was that what I was doing here? Pushing him away before he had a chance to leave too?

I blew out a slow breath. "Someone broke into my apartment and planted a yellow jacket like the one I saw on whoever ran out Speedy Zone's back door. That same person stole one of my work shirts, took a photo of someone dressed as me in front of Jake's house Monday night, the same night..." I looked around to make sure we were alone, but really, that wasn't a problem. I lowered my voice anyway though. "Well, you know. If someone thought I was hanging around outside his place, the police might also find evidence I was inside. This happened right after I met with the Anything Goes, who your Gran insisted I meet with Wednesday in my home. I was almost arrested yesterday, Travis, *and* followed a ways down Main Street. So yeah, I'm a little bit anti-trust at the moment."

All the color drained from his face while he stared at me. "Followed? What?" He swallowed hard. "I had no idea."

"No, I guess you wouldn't." Wait, that sounded like I believed him. He did seem sincere though. Still, it wasn't a good idea to trust anyone until I knew more.

Except Boxy. I could trust him. He was pulling into the parking lot and giving Travis major stink-eye.

"I'm really sorry this happened, Victoria," Travis said. "I'm leaving but only for work, not for good. If you need me, reach out." He half turned to leave as Boxy hobbled into the open garage. "I mean it, okay?"

Reluctantly, I nodded.

Boxy cowered away from Travis, hugging the side of the garage doorway, and held his cane out like a sword. "Be gone, fiend!"

"Keep an eye on her for me, Boxy," Travis said, ignoring Boxy's dramatics.

"Always do. Exactly one eye, and it's all for her." Boxy watched him drive away while I resumed inventory, or tried to. "Let me guess, he asked you to buy a timeshare *and* Speedy Zone and you still told him no? That man looked dejected."

"No timeshares. I accused him of framing me."

Boxy glared after him. "And did he?"

"I don't think so, which means I'm no closer to saving Sunray's." I sagged against the air filter shelf. "It's almost been a whole week without customers, and it's driving me bonkers."

"Hey, I get it." He caned his way closer and folded me into a one-armed hug. "But who says the responsibility is on you to save Sunray's? You're going to put yourself in an early grave doing what the police should be doing. For your safety and your sanity, you need to let them worry about it."

"But Sunray's is what I'm good at," I said into his shoulder.

"It's not going anywhere, and neither are you." He patted my back in little circles, which helped relieve some of my tension. "Now do you need any of Studmuffin's lemon macarons I smell before we get to searching Bernadette for clues?"

I'd texted him last night about what Detective Palmer told me.

I smiled. "I've already eaten six."

"That's my girl." He hugged me a little tighter and then pointed with his cane in the direction

Travis and his possessed car went. "One more question—do you like that boy or what?"

"'Or what' is the easier answer."

Boxy peered at me closer. "Is it the truth?"

"I don't know. Maybe." I'd have to sort out my feelings another day when I didn't have the urge to curl up into a little ball. Speaking of feelings though... "It's Friday, Boxy. Are you nervous for your date tonight with Ms. Stevenson?"

"Nervous? Me? Nah."

"So you're terrified, then?"

He laughed. "As a long-tailed cat in a room full of rocking chairs."

With a loud pop, Studmuffin appeared on the air filter shelf. As if imagining what Boxy had just said, he slapped his tail over Boxy's mouth.

"Right, no more talking," I said with a little chuckle. "Time to get to work."

ALL WE FOUND WAS a big fat zero. No dents or scratches or planted evidence in Bernadette of any kind. Everything that was supposed to be in my glove box was accounted for. We even searched the inside of the car vacuum for anything we might've missed. Nothing. My windshield wiper fluid was a little low, but that was the result of an extra buggy spring, not a murderer trying to frame me.

"At least Bernadette's looking extra spiffy now." Boxy vigorously rubbed some polish into my headlight.

I stepped back and admired the rest of her gleam. What a beauty. While we'd searched, we'd detailed the inside and out, right down to the hubcaps.

From his perch on his favorite shelf, Studmuffin was lazily judging a fly buzz into the garage, but I could already tell he was plotting to track paw prints over Bernadette's fresh wax sometime soon.

"Maybe I had this all wrong," I said. "Maybe this person wasn't following me at all. Maybe they were waiting for someone, not me, and just happened to be looking in my direction."

Boxy stood straight with the help of his cane. "But you said that Cass said that someone with ill intent was following you."

"Well, most of this town wishes me ill intent. It could've been anyone."

"That's why I'm going to give you something, and I'd like for you to take it." With his mouth twisted to the side, he fished inside his overalls pocket. He pulled out a small, black cylinder-shaped thing with a red flip-top cap. "You flip this cap up here, aim, and spray it at *anyone* with ill intent if they get too close. Keep it with you always."

"Pepper spray?" I took it from him but didn't dare to even touch the red cap. "And if I spray myself instead by mistake?"

"Don't do that," he warned. "I've been sprayed during training with it a time or two, and it's not pleasant. That was when I had both eyes for double the sting."

"This was during ninja training?"

"Obviously." He frowned as he looked at me. "I just hope you never have to use it, but if you find yourself in a bad situation, then use it."

"I will. Thanks, Boxy." Carefully, I tucked the gift I hoped I'd never have to use into my pocket.

WITH MY CAR INSPECTION and inventory done and absolutely nothing else to do, I decided to make a list. I sat at one of the cozy tables in the waiting area and used my favorite voice-to-text-message app on my phone. My favorite, because it could actually understand me. My plan was to name everyone I knew of who had contact with Jake and me in the last week and anything else I knew about them.

Travis Black – enough said. At Speedy Zone during murder.

Celeste – amazing eyeliner. At Speedy Zone during murder, but filling mop bucket and humming in the bathroom. Maybe laughing at something at Jake's funeral?

Gran Black – heavenly peach cobbler. Set up meeting with the AGs. Only trying to help?

The AGs, aka the Anything Goes – planted evidence inside my home? Knew about Jake's lost witchy heirloom?

Cherry Berenstein-- Jake's fiancée/not-fiancée. Owns a yellow jacket. Owns a light-gray Honda that could be mistaken for white. Might be crazy.

Kole Williams – Jake's uncle. Looked for lost heirloom inside Jake's house. Likes cute puppies.

This was probably an incomplete list, but since there were two people outside Speedy Zone after the murder, two of these people, or possibly even more, could be lying. But who?

I needed more information, and since it was almost dinnertime, I knew just the place to go—The Belly Up Diner. Weird name. Great food. Before Studmuffin, that was where I ate. Too bad for me it was definitely not calorie-free.

I burst into the garage where I found Boxy already glowering and his arms crossed as though he could read my mind.

"Vic..." he said.

"Boxy, I need to go."

"Need to go get into more trouble, you mean."

"I just need to ask Jake's fiancée a few questions, that's all. She's probably at The Belly Up working a shift. It's a public place. I'll go there and come straight back. I'll be fine." I patted his shoulder. "Would you like for me to get you anything?"

"Studmuffin's got me covered, but are you sure about this, Vic?"

"I'm sure I need answers. I plan on doing a little better about getting them this time," I said as I started toward Bernadette. "Call me after your date tonight?"

"I never kiss and tell."

"So you *are* planning on some kissing, then?" I grinned at the blooming flush in his cheeks. "Talk to you later. Behave yourself."

"Yeah..." Frowning, he halfheartedly waved. "You too."

THE LITTLE DINER BUSTLED with customers and wait staff when I walked in. It was busy even for a Friday night.

The smell of sizzling burgers, homemade French fries, and the secret spicy sauce the diner was known for made my stomach grumble.

It also smelled like onions. Whoever followed me down Main Street smelled like onions and ashes. This place was a smoke-free diner though. Still, though. Interesting.

It took me a bit to spot a free stool at the front counter. When Dad and I used to come here, which was a lot, we preferred the counter over the booths. Both of us liked to people watch, and this was the place to do it.

I squeezed between two burly men on either side of me. As soon as I sat, a waitress slapped a menu in front of me without a word and then walked off. Ah, good old Southern charm. Thankfully, the food here was much better than the service. While I waited for her to come back, I looked around for Cherry. I didn't see her.

When the waitress passed by for the fifth time without taking my order, I flagged her down. "Is Cherry Berenstein working tonight?"

"No," she snapped. "That's why we're short-staffed."

"Oh. Well, do you know where she is?"

"I don't know. She just ran off and left town." She grabbed a nearby coffee pot and refilled my burly neighbor's mug. "She said she didn't need to work anymore."

As in anywhere or just here? Now, why would she say that? If all of a sudden she didn't need to work, then that meant—

"Are you done?" The waitress tapped her foot. "I have customers."

Like me? I wanted to say, but I kept my mouth shut. The poor woman was doing her best.

"Thanks for your help," I told her and then left the diner to make a call.

"Yes, can I speak with Detective Palmer, please?" I asked the officer who answered.

"He's away from his desk right now."

"Can you have him call me as soon as he gets back?" I asked. "This is Victoria Fox."

"Sure, yeah, I can do that."

"Thanks." I hung up.

So where had Cherry run off to? Had she found Jake's heirloom and maybe pawned it to get the cash needed to quit her job?

I checked my phone for any pawn shops open right now. None were. Bummer.

If she'd had the heirloom, did that mean she killed Jake? Maybe it was all an act at Jake's house when she left for a double shift while dressed in her yellow jacket. Maybe she'd sent the detective a photo of "me" and then planted the evidence in my apartment. Now, she'd run off who knew where.

And she might just get away with murder.

Chapter Eighteen

There Are Vrooms, and Then There Are VROOMS

WHEN I GOT HOME from The Belly Up Diner, I found a pink, flower-perfumed envelope in my mailbox. The return address read Anything Goes.

My stomach sank. At the same time, a weird sense of hope made me hot and cold all over. I thought I wanted a coven to help me better myself as a witch, but I wasn't so sure the Anything Goes were for me. What if they were, though? I could adapt. Sort of. Okay, not really.

I returned to my apartment and cracked the window above the window seat. Already, the perfumey envelope gave me a headache. Inside, huge, loopy handwriting was scrawled across the pink paper. I sat down next to Studmuffin, who was arranged into a kitty loaf, and slowly began to decipher the words.

Dear Vitcoria (no joke—I read it six times, and that's still not how you spell my name),

We are sorry to inform you that Anything Goes is not the right coven for you. We are selective about the witches we allow into our coven, yet we welcome all with open hearts and arms. Feel free to contact us in six months if you have improved your craft.

Most sincerely,

Aster Perkins, High Priestess of Anything Goes

P.S. Get a broom.

My skin flushed as I reread the letter. *If* I have improved my craft, huh? *We are selective about witches, yet we welcome all?* Did they even care that made no sense? And yes, I would get a broom, but I doubted that would turn me into a proper witch the very next second. Not that I wanted to be proper, but still. Rejection stung.

"Don't worry, Studmuffin. I'll find another coven. Or maybe I won't. I've been doing just fine without doing magic for years."

I wasn't doing just fine, though, was I? I'd managed to run off all of Sunray's customers, and I wasn't sure there was any coming back from that. How great would it be if I could summon Jake's murderer to me, use my pepper spray, and then call Detective Palmer to come arrest them. Easy breezy.

Studmuffin gave me a stern, you-better-go-study expression.

"I'm on it, boss." Without a sleeping king to transport to The Place To Put Things I Don't Want To Think About Today, I got there much faster this time. My knees only trembled a little as I sat and cracked open my grimoire for the second time this week, a record for me lately.

I found the page for the summoning spell and read and reread it, noting the word now, not won, each time. Even if I did read that one word correctly, what if I jumbled up another and blew up the other half of the block? Right now, any explosions I caused would be exactly what I didn't need.

I must've waffled back and forth too long, because the next thing I knew, I jerked awake.

The sound of Studmuffin's murder mittens scrambled for purchase on the hardwood in the hallway. Then a ball of fur zipped past my chair. He knocked the other chairs out of his way and then bolted back down the hallway.

Oh yeah. He had a major case of the vrooms again.

As if to prove it, he howled. I swear he sounded more like a wolf than a cat. Shaking my head, I glanced at the old-fashioned clock above the microwave. Ten p.m. Too late for him to serenade me with the song of his species.

"Studmuffin, quiet," I hissed. "That's way too loud for this time of night."

He appeared at my side with a loud pop.

I screeched and nearly tipped out of my chair. "Enough. Put some brakes on yourself."

He lifted higher on his tiptoes, tilted his head, and pranced sideways like a drunk, dancing spider.

"What has gotten into you?"

The fur on his back spiked as he danced sideways in the other direction. Then he just...erupted. That's the only word I can think of to describe what he did next. Like he'd been shot out of a cannon straight into a tornado. He whisked by me and circled the table over and over. He went around so fast, whistling wind whipped my hair into the air.

"Stop!" I shrieked. "You're going to hurt yourself."

And then I heard it. Above the wind and the sounds of my crazy familiar, something else had the vrooms. An engine revved from right outside in the parking lot.

I recognized the sound of that purr. I recognized it because it was mine.

I shot up out of my chair. "Someone's stealing Bernadette!"

Studmuffin's luminescent eyes met mine as he whipped around the table. Then he went even faster. Two times as fast, maybe even three. I couldn't even see him anymore. The wind he created with his speed roared. It just about knocked me over. I gripped the edge of the table hard to keep upright.

"I need to go out there," I shouted. "Why are you doing this?"

Did he not want me to go outside? But I had to go. I had to stop my car from being stolen since she was one of the few things I had left.

I threw myself to the ground and army-crawled out of Studmuffin's vortex he was trying to trap me in. He must've been going too fast to notice because I was halfway to the door before the vortex slowed. Through the legs of the chairs underneath the table, I spied him spinning and stumbling in slow circles. The tip of his tongue poked out, and his eyes couldn't focus. He was either super dizzy or he really was a drunk, dancing spider.

"I have my phone and my pepper spray. I'll be fine," I said in a rush, then I bolted for the door.

Bernadette's engine revved louder as I bounded down the stairs. The poor girl wasn't used to being treated this way. Who was doing this? And how? I patted my pocket to make sure I still had my keys. Yep, still did.

I bolted out Sunray's front door and instantly noticed two things—no one sat behind the wheel and my trunk was open. What in the world? When I glanced through the driver's side window, I found a key in the ignition.

And then I knew. I gasped, the realization pulling me up short of the open trunk.

Key Kopies in Less Than 2 Minutes Guaran-keyed! That's what the poster inside Kole's Krafty Keys said, and I'd been parked right out front. Attached to Bernadette's rear wheel well was a magnetic key holder with an extra key inside. I'd put it there in case I locked myself out. I saw it just this morning when Boxy and I did our inspection, but I didn't think anything of it. The key inside had still been there. Had someone made a copy of it?

A single whispered footstep sounded behind me. Then pain exploded at the back of my head. Stars zipped past. I stumbled sideways, the second drunken spider of the night. What had hit me?

There was a loud pop. Two crying Studmuffins poofed into existence, but that wasn't right. I only had one familiar, thank goodness, and one was enough. I was seeing double.

The pain in my head throbbed as I tried to focus. Gingerly, I touched where I'd been smacked. My fingers came away sticky.

I had to get out of here.

"No more windy vortexes," I scolded the Studmuffin on the right. "Promise me."

"I knew you were crazy," an unfamiliar voice hissed from somewhere in the darkness.

Something rough shoved me. My feet lost the war with gravity. I flipped over into the open trunk. When I hit the inside, a fresh wave of agony dimmed all the lights inside my head.

I held my head so it wouldn't topple from my neck and pulled in a ragged breath. Why did my car smell like onions and ashes?

The trunk slammed down on top of me, sealing me in with the growing darkness hammering between my ears. Seconds later, the driver's side door clicked open and slammed shut. Then Bernadette and I vroomed away, neither of us by choice.

I swallowed hard and tried not to panic or pass out as my poor car's tires squealed around a corner. I fumbled for my phone in my back pocket, but it must've fallen out.

Far behind me, Studmuffin howled loud enough to wake the dead. In an instant, he popped inside the trunk with me, his velvet fur rubbing against my arm.

"Hey, I'm being kidnapped. This isn't the place for you," I told him.

He pawed my hair away from my eyes, but the onion smell must've gotten to him. He coughed and then howled and then poofed back out of the trunk.

"It's okay." I nodded, unsure if I was talking to my familiar who wasn't even here or myself. "It's fine. Everything's great."

And that's the last thing I said before I passed out.

Chapter Nineteen
Invisible Snowflakes

Awareness slipped through my mind slowly. It brought the crunch of tires over gravel one sharp rock at a time and ALL THE BUMPS. It might be obvious, but I wasn't a fan of trunk life.

For the first time in what seemed like a long time, Bernadette slowed. My stomach tightened. I'd lost track of time, so we could be anywhere—we meaning Bernadette, me, and our kidnapper. Whoever that was. When the trunk popped open again, I needed to have a plan. It was so hard to think straight with my knocked-around brain though.

To see what my options were like, I slid my hands over the rough carpet underneath me. Ah-ha! My phone! Good thing I hadn't dropped it. It provided enough light to see that I had zero signal. At the very least, I could snap a photo of whoever opened the trunk.

Unless I could open it first.

I knew cars, and I especially knew Bernadette. Inside most new-ish Pontiacs, there was a glow-in-the-dark emergency release latch. I'd never tried it because I'd never been knocked into a trunk that smelled like onions and ashes and kidnapped before. I'd spend the rest of my life trying to make sure I never got a chance to see if the latch worked again.

My car braked even more, nearly pulling to a stop. If I was going to escape, I had seconds.

My heartbeat thrashed between my temples and throbbed the pain in my head even more. I grasped the neon-green, T-shaped plastic handle on the inside of the trunk door and yanked it. The trunk popped open, but I gripped that T with all my strength so it wouldn't open even more. One glance in the rearview, and my kidnapper would surely suspect something when they saw the trunk open.

A sliver of daylight angled through the tiny crack. Daylight already? How long had I been in here?

Bernadette finally stopped. Time to go. Time to run, but then what? I didn't even know where I was. I needed to steal Bernadette back.

A plan as flimsy as chocolate pudding on the tip of Studmuffin's ear formed in my rattled brain. Yep, good enough.

The engine turned off.

I stashed my phone in my pocket, right next to my pepper spray. I slowly let go of the trunk, and as I did, I muttered, "Light, lighter, lightest. My arms are now featherweight. High, higher, highest. My body and spirit shall now levitate."

Magic exploded inside of me, the first I'd felt in years. Even better, it was working. I floated up out of the trunk toward the tops of several trees. We were in a secluded wooded area near a large lake that glimmered in the rising sun. Other than the morning birds chirping, Bernadette's tire tracks was the only other sign of life I could see, even ten feet off the ground. I kept going higher, steadying my breathing and angling myself behind a thick tree.

The driver's side door opened. A black-booted foot stepped out attached to a bare leg with shorts. That was similar to what I wore now. Then the rest of her appeared, complete with yellow jacket. A long turquoise ponytail trailed down her back. If I didn't know any better, I'd swear I was looking at myself. I couldn't see her face yet though.

She turned toward the open trunk and stopped. "Houston, we have a problem."

"Roger that," I whispered, keeping myself hidden. Did I know her from somewhere? It was impossible to tell.

"I can hear you breathing," she called, looking around.

Not possible. I'd stopped all lung action when she turned her head. I *did* know her. I'd recognize that perfectly winged eyeliner anywhere. It was the same woman from Speedy Zone, but she'd dyed her blonde hair turquoise. Travis had said her name was Celeste.

"I can feel you watching."

Yep, and I was about to take pictures so they'd last longer. I fumbled for my phone. Still no signal even twenty feet above the ground, but plenty of battery.

"I suppose you want to know why I brought you here."

It didn't take a genius to guess that one. I doubted it had anything to do with teaching me her makeup skills or announcing I was now the star of a reality survival show called *Levitating and Afraid*.

From behind the tree, I snapped several photos of her and her face. In one of them, something black and white streaked past Bernadette. Something with predator speed and silent agility.

Something super handsome.

Studmuffin to the rescue! Between the two of us, we'd definitely get me out of here alive. I grinned as he appeared on top of Bernadette right as the woman was passing by. She was too busy looking for me to even notice him, and she acted completely unaware when he swatted his murder mitten at her hair. The turquoise ponytail lifted from her head. A wig. She'd pinned her curly blonde hair to her head and had been wearing a wig.

Not anymore though. Turning, she patted her hair, her mouth drawn into an angry pout. Studmuffin and the wig had already vanished.

"You didn't say anything about her turning invisible," she shouted.

Wait, who was she talking to? I looked everywhere I thought I'd already looked then over my shoulder. My jaw dropped open. From this height, I saw that we weren't alone. Nestled in some thick bushes and hidden behind several fallen logs sat a white car. *The* white car? It was hard to tell. But where was the driver?

Quickly, I snapped more photos.

"Can't you just find her already and get it over with?" Celeste shouted.

Absolutely not.

When I turned back around, Celeste scrambled to catch my familiar. He ran off with her wig between his fangs. It would have been quite a funny sight if it had been any other person at any other time. The rage on her face spelled trouble though. She dive-bombed him, sliding on the leaves and dirt straight toward Bernadette's driver's side door. Studmuffin expertly tiptoed out of the way, but Celeste didn't, or couldn't, stop. She banged her head on my car and slumped to the ground.

"Yes," I whispered and fist-bumped the tree I hid behind. If, you know, trees had fists to bump. My own head might have been hit harder than I thought.

A victorious gleam brightened Studmuffin's eyes as he turned to look at me. Then he froze. His gaze aimed behind me, twenty feet off the ground, and he howled.

My body began to piece together what would happen next before my brain caught up. I whirled, my fingers already seeking the pepper spray in my pocket.

You flip this cap up here, aim, and spray it, Boxy had said.

That's exactly what I did as the rest of what was happening fell into place. Aster Perkins, High Priestess of the AGs, levitated behind me. Her face was twisted in a ferocious scowl.

"You *do* have a car," I blurted.

She rolled her eyes. "Yes, let's talk about *that* right now."

Her fist shot toward me, a large ring banded around her index finger's first knuckle. A dark blue sphere no bigger than a marble suspended in the middle of tiny silver clouds. The Ring of Everlasting Night. Its power prickled into my skin.

We struck at the same time—me with my pepper spray, her with her rocket fist.

Pain. A whole lot of it while Aster shrieked. I plummeted down, down, down twenty feet. It was a long way, plenty of time for me to say the levitation spell again if I hadn't had the sense knocked out of me for the second time in less than a day. It was such a long way that I must've passed out again. Was I falling in slow motion or through the center of the earth or what?

An engine purred to life below, moved right underneath me, and then sat idling. As though I were an invisible snowflake, I floated through the top of the car and into Bernadette's passenger seat. The seat belt clicked around me.

"Thanks," I mumbled. "Safety first."

I thought I was conscious, at least sort of, but next to me in the driver's seat sat Studmuffin. His murder mittens lay exactly at ten and two on the steering wheel as we raced away from Celeste and Aster.

So, this was now a thing. My familiar could drive.

"How are you even reaching the gas pedal?" I blinked hard at the footwell underneath him. Easy. He wasn't. Yet we were flying out of there. "Slow down!"

The wind breezed through his fur, and all he needed to complete the confident-roadster look was a pair of kitty sunglasses. Completely ignoring me, he careened us onto a narrow dirt road and knocked me into the passenger door.

"Oof." My head didn't like that. Neither did my stomach. Okay, no more looking at where we were going. Or thinking about how my cat had lead toe beans. Or knowing he didn't need to touch his tootsies to the pedal.

So I just let the weirdness happen and drifted off like the snowflake I was.

Chapter Twenty

Swatting Cotton Candy Clouds

"Oh, I THINK SHE'S coming around."

The familiar voice seeped through cotton candy clouds flecked with chocolate sprinkles. From somewhere, a stomach growled. Pretty sure it was mine, but everything was still a little fuzzy.

"Well, maybe…"

That was Boxy. I thought I felt his hand in mine, but my arms felt detached from the rest of me. So did my legs. And my head. Wow, that was some image to gain consciousness to.

"Here," I muttered as though I were answering roll call.

"How do you feel?"

"Well…" I croaked. "I can't see anything."

He sighed. "Your eyes are closed, Vic."

"Oh, I knew that." I cracked open one, and bright white hospital light poured in and blinded me. "*Oh.* I think I'll keep them closed. I feel too floaty."

He patted my hand with his other one. "That must be the drugs they gave you."

Some drugs. My back teeth were floating.

"Where's Studmuffin?" I asked.

"On your face," Boxy said matter-of-factly.

I smiled into what I realized was his fur, not cotton candy. It was hard to tell because my whole face was numb. "Hey, handsome."

He licked my cheek with his rough tongue, and his big motor revved from deep inside him.

"The doctors and nurses had quite a time trying to pry him off you. They quickly learned who's boss, though, when the claws came out." Boxy laughed. "Paws out, claws out. Am I right, buddy?"

I felt Studmuffin lift his mitten for a fist-to-paw bump.

"Thanks for saving me, my little hero," I told him.

"That he is." Boxy fell quiet for a moment. "You were in pretty bad shape, Vic. No concussion thankfully, but your nose is very broken. You've also got a knot on the back of your head the size of a grapefruit. There for a little bit, I thought I was going to have to bring a piñata to your funeral."

That forced my eyes open, the light now the least of my pains since what he'd just said had brutally attacked my heart. His one good eye was sad and tired-looking, and what was left of his silver hair stuck up all over the place. He looked like he'd slept in a running dryer.

"There's never any reason to worry about me, Boxy. You know as well as anyone how hard my head is. Remember sixth grade? The field trip to the science museum? I fell off the wooden castle and landed right on my head."

That was before I'd learned to levitate. Not good times.

"The bounce heard around the world." He chuckled, but it didn't have his usual Boxy glee to it. "It's in my nature to worry about you though. I should've been there with you last night watching scary movies. You said someone was following you, and instead of protecting you, I went on a coffee date."

"Which is exactly where you should've been," I assured him. "You can't live life being afraid something bad *might* happen."

He lifted his eyebrows. "Wise words."

"I have my moments." I squeezed his hand, so grateful he was by my side. "So, what happened? I mean, I remember some things, but the sugar-rotted holes in my brain are now plugged with cotton candy and cat fur and drugs and... What was I saying?"

Wow, I was loopy.

"I only know about the face-hugger hero you've got there," he said, stroking Studmuffin down his back, "but Detective Palmer has been hovering since he got here. I'm sure he'll pop in sooner rather than later."

"He can't arrest me. I'm sure I have proof emblazoned on my nose that I didn't steal Jake's missing heirloom and more proof on my phone."

Boxy nodded. "He knows that by now. All *I* know is what Studmuffin there told me, and the rest I figured out for myself."

"He told you, huh?" I sighed and scratched my stubborn familiar behind the ears, which made him curl up around my face even tighter.

"Yeah, he said you took a ride in the back of Bernadette's trunk and that it smelled like onions and ashes. I've never taken a ride in a trunk myself. How was it?"

"It's exactly how you might imagine it. Zero out of ten. Would not recommend. Please, go on."

"He said Celeste drove you out to Carter Lake. He found her intentions on what to do with you there in the form of a letter in Bernadette's passenger seat." He winced at that last part.

"What did the letter say?"

"That you murdered Jake and were sorry." He sat back in his chair and rubbed his temples, spiking his silver hair even more. "So sorry that you were going to drive yourself into the lake with the car windows down with your confession letter pinned to a nearby tree."

"Whoa. Good thing it didn't get that far."

He nodded. "Good thing indeed. That lady, Celeste, from Speedy Zone and Aster Perkins were desperate to get themselves off the hook. From the little Detective Palmer has told me, he was closing in on them fast though."

"I knew he was smarter than he looked." I shrugged one shoulder. "Well, not really, but I'm happy to be proved wrong about him."

As if his ears had been tingling, the detective himself knocked gently on the door as he entered. "Oh, good. You're awake. Feeling up to some questions?"

Boxy chuckled. "You're not one to waste any time, are you, Detective?"

He started to turn away. "I can come back."

"No, Detective, it's fine," I said. "I have some questions of my own."

He closed the door, smiling slightly. "I wouldn't expect anything less coming from you."

Was that a compliment? Without an accusation behind it, and said with a hint of warmth, it sure sounded like he was complimenting me.

Boxy caught my eye, and his caterpillar eyebrows climbed his forehead. He'd noticed too.

"So." Detective Palmer settled himself in the chair next to my bed opposite Boxy. He clasped his hands across his lean belly. He looked slightly more relaxed than I'd ever seen him without his tie and the top two buttons undone on his black shirt. "You didn't kill Jake."

"No. I was innocent all along." I narrowed my eyes at him. "I bet you knew that before I was knocked into a trunk last night, right?"

He frowned. "That's right. The forensic report came back on that yellow jacket we found at your place, and there were a few hairs on it, all synthetic."

"A wig."

The detective nodded. "Likely the same one Celeste wore in the pictures you took."

Boxy leaned forward in his chair and wagged his finger at the detective. "Something tells me you knew Vic was innocent even before that."

"I had my suspicions, yes. The motive didn't quite fit. If Victoria wanted to hurt Speedy Zone, she wouldn't go after Jake. Travis Black would've been the target. It just makes sense given both your families' history."

Boxy glowered and started to open his mouth, probably to say something like, "There's still time," but I cut him off.

"I was there at Speedy Zone that night though. I have the know-how to disassemble the relief valve on a hydraulic lift."

"So did Celeste," Detective Palmer said. "It turns out she was the one who drove Aster's car away from the back of Speedy Zone. She hid it behind the church across the street and ran back into work before her mop bucket had filled."

"But..." I swatted the cotton candy clouds away so I could think straighter. "I heard her humming."

"That came from her phone to help give her a solid alibi," the detective said with a nod. "It was Aster dressed in the yellow jacket who actually committed the murder. Celeste told her how."

Whoa. Aster had been in my home. I'd thought about joining her coven. A shiver swept through my numb body.

"But why?" I asked. "Why kill Jake?"

The detective sighed. "He mentioned the heirloom to Celeste. Shortly after, it went missing. He confronted her. She begged him not to tell Travis for fear he'd fire her if he found out she was stealing from other employees. She told Jake she'd give it back. When she didn't, he threatened to go to Travis. Apparently that's when it was decided that this heirloom was worth more than Jake's life."

Nothing could ever be that important though. Nothing.

"Which one broke into my apartment?" I asked.

"That was Celeste. It was Aster you saw on Main Street. She made a copy of your car key at Kole's Krafty Keys. Kole remembered her clearly because his dog kept growling at her."

"Smart Killer."

The detective frowned. "Hmm?"

"Kole's puppy. His name is Killer, even though it doesn't fit him."

"I see," he said, rubbing his chin. "Aster saw you in front of Kole's, and that's where she hatched the plan to drive you and your car into the lake. All she needed was a copy of your car key, so she did a locator spell."

A locator spell? He'd said that so matter-of-factly. So he *did* know about magic and witches. Did he know about me too?

"Does Aster smoke?" I asked, remembering what Cass had said. The person with ill intent who'd followed me smelled like ashes and onions.

Detective Palmer's brow wrinkled. "Yes, why?"

"Does she eat a lot of onions?"

"I don't know, but she lives with her sister who works at The Belly Up Diner," he said. "What is this about?"

"My trunk smelled like onions," I told him.

Boxy snapped his fingers. "Cats hate onions. She must've made it smell that way on purpose. She knew about Studmuffin."

I nodded. "Jake's fiancée, Cherry, worked at The Belly Up. Is Cherry Aster's sister? I was trying to call you about her last night."

"No," the detective answered. "But Cherry's the reason I didn't get your call last night. She skipped town, so I followed. She said she and Jake were planning to elope and move into her house. It turns out she was right. Jake wrote up a will, declaring his car, house, and savings should all go to his future wife, Cherry Berenstein. Apparently that was all finalized the day he died. They were going to elope the very next day."

It was so sad they didn't get to. It also explained Jake's appointment with Boro Yate, the lawyer, written on his calendar. I'd bet Boro helped write the will or signed it as a witness. The haircut at Henderson's Barbershop shortly before that appointment was so he'd look his best for his wedding day. Poor Cherry. I couldn't imagine how she might be feeling right now.

"But," the detective continued with a sigh, "it turns out Celeste and Aster picked the wrong person to frame though."

"Hear, hear." Nodding, Boxy clasped his hands together as though praying to the car gods.

"Have they been arrested?" I asked.

"And charged," Detective Palmer said. "They both confessed everything back at the station. After Boxy called 911, we found Celeste passed out at the lake. Aster was still suffering the effects of pepper spray there too."

I breathed a sigh of relief. "It's always a good day when someone's been locked up for murder and attempting to murder me too."

"More good days await, then," Boxy said with a grin.

The detective firmed his mouth into a thin line. "There are a couple things bothering me about how you got yourself back to Belle's Cove in the shape you were in."

I opened my mouth to answer and then slowly closed it again. Umm, how to answer that? Admit that I'm a witch and that my familiar knows how to drive? Detective Palmer might think I was innocent of murder but nuttier than a fruitcake if I admitted that. Besides, as far as I was aware, Studmuffin didn't have a license.

"Vic," Boxy whispered, leaning forward, "it might help to know that the detective noticed the broom in the corner as soon as he came in here."

I frowned, trying to turn my head toward the corner, but Studmuffin was hugging my face too tightly. "Which broom?"

"Exactly," Boxy said with a nod.

"No, I mean which..." And then I spotted it behind several huge vases filled with flowers. It was leaning against the corner by the bathroom. "Oh. *Witch* broom."

A bundle of sticks poked from the top of a long, sturdy-looking, though delightfully crooked, handle. Blue and yellow ribbons that were the exact same colors as Sunray's waiting area secured the sticks to the handle in pretty bows. My vision was still fuzzy, but it looked like little cars decorated the ribbons. It was the most thoughtful gift anyone had ever made for me, and it was absolutely perfect.

Detective Palmer cleared his throat, and I realized I still hadn't answered his question. "Yes, I am aware what you are, Ms. Fox. I also know all about the Anything Goes and the other covens in town."

"I see." Part of me wanted to ask him which coven he thought might be the best fit for me. Now wasn't the time, though, and here wasn't the place. "To answer your question about how I got back to town... See the scarf around my neck? He's my familiar. He bakes. He bosses. He burns rubber down highways. His name is Professor Studmuffin Salvitore III, and he saved my life."

An almost smile slanted across the detective's mouth as he regarded my cat. Then, as if he'd been holding himself back, he sprang his hand out to grasp mine. His warm touch tingled up my arm.

"It's not every day I meet a hero," he said earnestly. "What you and your familiar did out at that lake was very brave. You never gave up to prove your innocence. Not once."

I had no idea what to say to that. I didn't feel like a hero. I didn't correct him, either, or move my hand out from underneath his.

A strange silence fell between us while our eyes stayed locked. His fingers lingered on mine. Then, seeming to catch himself, he pulled away and rose quickly.

"Try to stay out of trouble, Ms. Fox. I hope you feel better soon." Turning, he rushed from the room like his shoes had caught fire.

I blinked after him. "Okay... Did he seem...different?"

Boxy nodded. "That must be how he acts when he's not treating you like a suspect and possibly one day might want to treat you to coffee."

"What?" My head hurt too much to think or process or pretty much everything else.

"Nothing," Boxy said with a secret smile. "Just that I doubt that's the last we'll see of Detective Palmer."

I gasped. "Coffee!"

"As in you'd like some?"

"As in your date. How was it? Tell me everything."

"Fine." Boxy shrugged as if it was no big deal, but his flushed cheeks and broad grin gave him away.

"Boxy..."

His grin brightened even more and filled the room. "Simply amazing."

"I *knew* it. When's the wedding?"

He held up his hands. "Well, now, let's not get carried away. Date number two is a picnic in the park Sunday afternoon."

"So soon after date number one?" I whistled low. "Boxy, I'm impressed."

"If you need me to look after you on Sunday, though, I'll—"

"Nope." I shook my head. I wouldn't dream of a little broken nose and bump on the head keeping Boxy away from another date. "All I need is for you to go on a picnic with Ms. Stevenson. A happy Boxy equals a happy Vic."

He chuckled. "While a happy Vic *is* important, I'll settle for an alive Vic any day."

My chest warmed from within, and without. Studmuffin melted into liquid form as he dozed harder and slid farther down my torso. Rescuing me must've really tuckered him out.

"Did Cass bring all these flowers and the balloon?" I asked softly so I wouldn't wake him.

"The huge vase of red roses that are screaming desperation are from He Who Only Comes Out At Night," Boxy explained. "The single yellow rose and balloon are from me. The leafy ones wrapped in brown paper are from Cass, and of course the broom. She said to tell you she's sticking around for a while to make sure you're okay."

I grinned. Thank goodness she hadn't left yet. "The leafy ones" Boxy had mentioned looked like thistle, eucalyptus, and baby's breath, and the pretty yellow and blue ribbons tied around the brown paper had cars printed on them, too, just like my broom.

My broom. It had never occurred to me to get one because I loved cars so much, but now... Well, mine was pretty spectacular.

"Do you think Bernadette will be jealous I have a broom now?" I asked.

Boxy waved that question away. "Nah, that's not how she rolls. Just don't forget about her."

"Never."

Using his cane, Boxy pushed to his feet. "Want to see it? She left a note with it."

"Sure."

He hobbled over to the corner where it leaned. "I'm no expert with brooms, but this one looks like a keeper."

"It's beautiful," I agreed and took it from him when he handed it to me.

It was shockingly lightweight, like holding air. The magic thrumming through it dashed up my fingertips and skipped toward my heart, joining us together.

"We'll have to get you a parachute or a really large trampoline while you learn to ride that thing." Concern tinged Boxy's voice. I knew he wouldn't let me out of his sight with it, at least until I could prove I knew what I was doing. Which could be a while.

I opened the little brown envelope tucked into the bundle of sticks. The neat, handwritten letters swam over the page, but eventually I focused and pinned them down.

Victoria,

It tastes pink. Sorry!

Feel better soon,

Casserole Rudio

I showed the note to Boxy. He confirmed I wasn't crazy when his eyes widened as he read.

"Pink has a taste?" He blinked hard at me.

"Ummmm....?" I shrugged. "Maybe more importantly, does this mean I have to *eat* the broom?"

Chapter Twenty-One
No Brooms Were Harmed or Eaten. Yet.

THE HOSPITAL KEPT ME for another twenty-four hours and then released me. It took me about another week to feel like myself again though. During that time, I healed my mind, body, and soul and loved on Studmuffin extra hard. He allowed it, which was a bonus.

Boxy said that business at Sunray's was picking up again. I desperately wanted to be back in the shop, but both Boxy and my familiar kept me away. They knew best, especially since deep down, I still felt rattled about everything that happened, and could have happened, at the lake. I was still here, though, still standing. For that, I was grateful.

It was early on a Monday morning when a familiar-sounding possessed car screeched into the parking lot. Boxy hadn't yet arrived, so that left

Studmuffin and me to deal with He Who Only Comes Out at Night. Actually that left me to deal with him since my familiar was already nodding off at the sound of Travis's cowboy boots.

I opened one of the garage doors to greet him—and to apologize. With The Ring of Everlasting Night still faintly tattooed into my nose, and Celeste and Aster behind bars, it was pretty obvious he didn't have anything to do with Jake's murder.

"Hey." He stopped short, a broad smile on his face, and stuck his hands into his jeans pockets. He wore a white T-shirt that showed off his tan, and the rising sun gave his sandy-blond hair a reddish hue. "How are you feeling?"

"More...attached, I guess is the right word. My brain is growing back nicely, and so is my nose." I shrugged. "I had no idea I was part starfish, but there you go."

He chuckled and then peered closer. "Yeah, your nose looks real nice."

Studmuffin trotted up to him and then promptly plopped down and fell asleep on his left boot.

"Hey, bud," Travis said to him and got a loud snore in response.

"Travis," I began, "I'm really sorry."

"I just wanted to say how sorry I am," he said at the exact same time. "Oops. Ladies first."

I laughed awkwardly. "I, uh... I had no right to accuse you of murder. That was out of line. I think maybe I wanted it to be you so I could continue hating you, but...you're not your dad. I'm sorry I didn't realize that sooner."

"You don't have to apologize. I would've thought the same thing." Frowning, he stared down at the glowing ring on his hand. Now that he wasn't hiding it, the differences between it and the Ring of Everlasting Night were obvious. It was a lighter shade of blue suspended in the middle of twinkling silver stars, not clouds. "There's something I should tell you."

"Okay..." Uh-oh. Was this part where he admitted he *was* a killer? Or that he really was just like his dad? Or that—*gasp*—1980s station wagons with wood paneling were ugly? Because they aren't. They're classic.

"Gran and I..." He twisted the ring back and forth. "We're vampires."

My starfish brain that hadn't quite finished growing back had to reboot for that one. "Huh?"

"You're the first person I've told." He blew out a rush of air. "I didn't want to tell you at first, but then you admitted you were a witch so freely. I wished that I could do that. I didn't quite know how you'd react though." He peered closer at me. "How *are* you reacting?"

"Um..." I shrugged, not knowing what else to do or say. "How are you a vampire?"

He shook his head and gazed down at Studmuffin on his boot. "It happened by accident."

"You mean you and your gran tripped and fell onto a vampire's fangs or...?"

He snorted. "No, it didn't happen quite like that. We needed help with the farm, and I needed help with Speedy Zone. We couldn't do it all, so Gran said she knew someone who could help."

"A vampire?"

"No, a coven here in town. *Not* Anything Goes. They're called The Crow and Switch."

"Oh." I filed that name away in case they were worth checking out. "Is this coven a bunch of vampires?"

"No, not that I know of. Anyway, they whipped up a little potion for us so that Gran and I wouldn't need to sleep."

I nodded. "Like vampires. They don't need sleep."

"Exactly, only we drank too much of the potion. We were supposed to drink one sip over several days, not all at once. Gran heard them wrong, and I wasn't there when the instructions were given. Let's just say the result was bad. Real bad. Blood Boils, the witches called it. The only way to ease it was to have a vampire bite us...and turn us."

"Wow. I'm sorry." I was saying that a lot lately, but it was true.

He shrugged like it was no big deal. "What's funny, only not really, is now I'm constantly tired. I can't sleep, though, which means I have more time to do things at the shop and the farm. The coven felt so bad about everything that they gave Gran and me these rings to let us walk around during the day. They call them The Rings of Everlasting Sunblock."

I'd have to see if those rings were mentioned in my grimoire later. If they were in there, they'd likely be on the page *after* The Ring of Everlasting Night. "So, you drink blood? And apparently cobbler too? I mean you *eat* cobbler too?"

"There's this synthetic kind of blood that tastes just like strawberries. Gran and I sometimes drizzle it on top of cobbler, because even death can't stop us from eating that."

My eyes widened. "Yeah, I guess this does mean you're dead." A part of me wanted to reach out and feel his heartbeat, or lack of one rather, but I stopped myself. "He Who Only Comes Out At Night."

A frown twitched his mouth. "Sorry?"

"That's what Boxy and I called you. Still do sometimes, but it's like I knew this already because you only came out at night. I mean you used to come out at night."

He nodded. "Then we got the rings." He stepped closer with the foot not pinned down by my snoring familiar. "Does this...change anything? Between us, I mean."

"Between an accidental vampire auto shop owner and a reluctant witch auto shop owner?" I shook my head. "We're not all that different."

His shoulders loosened in relief, and a wide smile lit up his entire face. "Good. I'm glad you think so. My ex-fiancée wasn't as understanding as you about the whole vampire thing...or as honest as you about anything. I think I always knew it wouldn't work out between us and why I never introduced her to Gran."

"Well, she missed out on some good cobbler," I said.

He laughed. "So she did..."

Our gazes caught and held for a long moment.

But then I cleared my throat. "So Jake's ring, the heirloom from his grandmother... Since you're a bit of a witchy ring expert now, do you know much about The Ring of Everlasting Night?"

"Only a little. Gran and I flipped past that section in a witch grimoire we borrowed from The Crow and Switch to read more about The Rings of Everlasting Sunblock. It sounds like this heirloom is very powerful."

"Must be if Celeste and Aster thought it was worth killing Jake over."

"You know Mrs. Salmon of Salmon Ridge Estates? Belle's Cove's biggest gossip?"

"I've heard of her, yes."

"How she knows this, I don't know, but she told Gran that Celeste wanted to join the Anything Goes. Celeste told them that Jake told *her* he had a mysterious heirloom and described what it looked like. Celeste immediately knew what it was. So did Aster. Aster told Celeste to find and get the ring for not only entry into her coven, but a *special* place in the coven. Whatever that means. Celeste did a summoning spell, the ring disappeared from Jake's candle, and I think you know the rest of the story."

I rolled my eyes skyward. "So when Aster says Anything Goes, what she really means is murder."

He shrugged. "Gran and I didn't know any of this before now, I swear. If we had, we would've steered you *far* away from that coven. Gran feels terrible. So do I. If you weren't standing here today..." He blew out a long breath. "I'm really glad you are."

"Me too." I smiled at him to put his worries at ease. It was the least I could do after accusing him of murder. "Have you found a buyer for Speedy Zone?"

"Not yet." He narrowed his hazel eyes, a quizzical smile on his mouth. "Why? You know someone who's interested?"

"Nope." Not yet anyway. Maybe someday.

A black Ford pickup truck pulled up behind Travis's Mustang, but the rising sun created too much of a glare off the windshield to see who it was.

Please let it be a customer. Right after I thought that, another car rolled to a stop in front of the second garage, and yet another in front of the third.

My jaw dropped to my knees. Were these all customers? Like, the paying kind?

Travis leaned toward me, careful of Studmuffin. "I think this might be the first time I've ever seen you speechless."

"I—" I caught the sheepish grin on his face. "Did you have something to do with this?"

"Boxy let it slip to Ms. Stevenson who told Gran who told me that this would be your first day back." He shrugged one shoulder. "I may have let it slip to one or two fans of yours."

A dog yipped from the pickup and sprang out of the driver's side. It didn't get very far with the leash around its neck. Kole followed after it and waved.

"Not Killer! Kole! Great to see you," I gushed.

When the others stepped out of their cars, my heart nearly leaped out of my chest. It was Jake's parents and two younger sisters, all of whom waved and seemed perfectly comfortable being here.

It took all my will to keep the tears at bay as I turned back to Travis. "Thank you."

His smile softened a bit. "It's the least I could do."

"Then can I start with *your* car?" I said. "I'll go grab the holy water and a demon trap."

He threw back his head and laughed. "It's a deal. I hope you're ready to get to work."

"I am." I practically skipped to the waiting area door to usher everyone inside, hoping that Studmuffin had prepared enough desserts since it was never too early for cake. One glance through the postage-stamp window, and I could tell he'd delivered and then some. "I really, really am."

Chapter Twenty-Two
Fluffer-Stinker

So, I'd been doing a lot of thinking. Between exorcising the demon from Travis's Mustang and a steady trickle of returning, sometimes sheepish, customers, my mind had been in a constant spin about my choices, my life, and my future.

A wise woman named Victoria Fox once said, "You can't live life being afraid something bad *might* happen." True, she'd been hopped up on painkillers at the time, but I remembered those words clear as day. It was because I was afraid something bad might happen that I'd turned my back for so long on who I am—a witch. No one ever said I had to be a perfect one. Plus, I had a witch's familiar whom I wasn't so sure I deserved if I wasn't, you know, a witch.

On top of that, when Travis had made the offer to me to buy Speedy Zone, he'd reawakened a dream. I'd slowly let this dream die, because yet again, I was afraid something bad would happen. Like I'd fall flat on my face. Like I'd fail. The truth was I imagined going to college since the end of my junior year in high school when the guidance counselor handed me a stack of pamphlets and applications.

"Apply," she'd told me. "I see great things for you, Victoria." Maybe she was a psychic or maybe she was just doing her job. I didn't know. But a business degree would help give me the confidence and a sturdy foundation to build up from. To grow and spread, like the first sunrays over the horizon.

Was I up to it?

Well, I'd survived a little murder attempt and helped put some baddies in jail, something I thought I'd never do. Nearly dying sure put things into perspective. But being a witch and going to college had to be easier than all that, right?

The Anything Goes also helped me take a good, hard look at myself. Even before their High Priestess tried to murder me. I would remain a stagnant puddle if I kept living my life this way. Not that there was anything wrong with that. But I could be so much more, if I wanted to.

The question was—did I?

Taking a big gulp of air, I crossed toward The Place To Put Things I Don't Want To Think About Today.

"I see you, too, broom," I told it as I passed by where it leaned against the couch. Apparently I talk to my broom now. I hadn't touched it and/or tasted it since I brought it home from the hospital. "One very small step at a time."

Nervously tapping my phone, I sat in front of my grimoire and the application to the University of Georgia. Yes, I could submit it online, but talking out my essay answers in my voice-to-text app first would help me take my time and sort out my thoughts first. When I was satisfied, I'd transfer my answers online.

Check it out. I had a plan, and I wasn't even hyperventilating.

I skipped the basics like name and birthday and went right to the first real essay question. *Why do you want to attend The University of Georgia?* I made sure the app was going on my phone and began my answer.

What sounded like a ball smashing into bowling pins echoed from down the hall. I gasped and froze solid. Four little feet scrambled around the wooden floor, trying to get purchase and failing miserably. Finally, Studmuffin skidded down the hallway on his bottom. His eyes were wider than I'd ever seen them and glued to mine.

"What are you doing?" I screeched.

He kept on sliding. At the last second, he tucked into a roll before he crashed into the front door. Before I could applaud his acrobatics or run to see if he was all right, he did something I never expected. But always wondered if he might someday...

He struck a power pose, poofed out his white chest, fixed me with his sternest professor glare, and opened his mouth to say, "It's about time you filled that out, young lady."

If you enjoyed reading this book, please consider leaving a review!
Don't miss the rest of the series:

- *Hisses, Hearses, & Curses: Witchy Business Book 2*

- *Purrs, Chauffeurs, & Saboteurs: Witchy Busi-*

ness Book 3

- *Corvettes, Amulets, & Suspects: Witchy Business Book 4*

- *Paws, Laws, & Santa Claws: Witchy Business Book 5*

About the Author

Maddy Savanna writes cozy paranormal mysteries. This basically means she knows where all the best places are to bury bodies. If you bribe her with chocolate, chances are good she'll tell you where. A self-described book witch, she also writes stories under two other pen names. She dreams of being a cat when she finally grows up.

Check out her website at: www.maddysavanna.com